D0975305

rhcbooks.com

ISBN 978-0-7364-4242-8 (hardcover)
ISBN 978-0-7364-4241-1 (paperback)

Printed in the United States of America

10 9 8 7 6 5 4 3

# DISNEY
# ENCANTO

The Deluxe Junior Novelization

Adapted by Angela Cervantes

Random House 🏠 New York

The golden glow of the candle filled the room as a young girl and her grandma huddled close together. The flame danced off the young girl's oversize glasses as she kept her eyes shut.

"Abre los ojos . . . ," said the abuela, gazing lovingly at her granddaughter. "Open your eyes."

The young girl, named Mirabel, opened both eyes and saw a wondrous, magical candle rippling with firelight magic. "This is where our magic comes from?" she asked her abuela.

"Mm-hmm, this candle holds the miracle given to our family."

"How did we get a miracle?"

Abuela folded an arm around Mirabel's shoulder, and the candle glowed brighter. As Abuela began the story of the miracle, Mirabel could see it unfold in each flick of the flame: In their humble home, young Abuela Alma and her husband, Pedro, gazed down in adoration at their three newborn babies. On a table nearby, the same candle glimmered gently.

Suddenly, a harsh blaze exploded outside their home. The young couple's adoring smiles disappeared.

"Long ago, when my three babies had just been born, your abuelo Pedro and I were forced to flee our home."

Pedro, holding the candle, led a group of frightened people as they struggled across a beautiful river.

"And though many joined us, hoping to find a *new* home, we could not escape the dangers . . . and your abuelo was lost."

Abuela's eyes shimmered in the candlelight as she recalled the night her young family fled the violence that had swept through their town.

As Mirabel listened to her grandma's story,

she snuggled close, worried for the families. She could see them as they crossed a river together. Suddenly, Pedro glanced back. His hopeful gaze turned troubled. Danger had followed them, and he had no choice but to face it and protect his family. He looked lovingly into his wife's eyes, handed her the candle, and left to confront the threat.

The candle's flame dwindled, and darkness drew closer. Young Abuela knew that something terrible had happened. Pedro was not coming back.

Filled with grief, she knelt by the river and prayed with the candle in front of her. When all seemed lost, the candle suddenly flickered alive, bright and strong. And then butterflies, full of light, swirled and banished the darkness. The earth rumbled and mountains rose, forming a protective valley around the families.

"The candle became a magical flame that could never go out, and it blessed us with a refuge in which to live. A place of wonder . . . an Encanto," Abuela said. "The miracle grew, and our house, our Casita itself, came alive to shelter us."

Young Abuela's prayers had been answered. The candle grew brighter, and from the earth, a magnificent house formed. She found herself and her triplets in the courtyard of a spectacular casa that was as alive as they were! It welcomed them by flapping its window shutters. The tiny babies squealed in amazement.

"When my children came of age, the miracle blessed each with a magic gift to help us," Abuela Alma continued. "And when *their* children came of age—"

"They got magic, too!" Mirabel interrupted, smiling excitedly.

Mirabel saw the three babies, now five years old, each in front of their own door. The magic candle guided them to receive their special gifts. As they touched the doorknobs, a bright light radiated, filling each of them with a magical gift. The house quickly created bedrooms that matched their special gifts.

"That's right. And together, their magical gifts have made our community a paradise."

With the magic, the wilderness that surrounded

the house transformed into a land of sunshine. Tall wax palm trees stretched toward the blue sky, and lush fruit trees and colorful flowers bloomed all year long. And it all started with Abuelo Pedro's sacrifice to protect the family.

Mirabel stared in awe at the candle. How could something so small be so powerful?

Her abuela snuggled her, bursting with pride. "Tonight, this candle will give you *your* gift, mi vida. Strengthen our community, strengthen our home. Make your family proud."

"Make my family proud," Mirabel repeated with a steady voice.

Fireworks exploded outside, and the house signaled that it was time to begin.

"Yes, yes, Casita, we're going," Abuela chuckled.

The house slid Mirabel her shoes. It was as excited as she was for this big moment. As Abuela and Mirabel paused in front of the door, they held hands.

"What do you think my gift will be?" Mirabel asked Abuela.

Abuela bent down to Mirabel. "You are a

wonder, Mirabel," she said, oozing love and pride. "Whatever gift awaits will be just as special as you."

Mirabel held the candle in her tiny hands. She could feel the warmth and possibility. She was ready to receive her gift and make her family proud!

# Chapter
# One

Years later, fifteen-year-old Mirabel woke up early, eager to tackle the special day. There was so much that needed to be done for her little primo's gift day! As she hurried around her room to get herself dressed, the house could barely keep up! It slid her shoes and green-rimmed glasses in her direction but barely caught her nightgown as she quickly changed into her embroidered skirt and blouse. Now she was ready!

The bedroom door opened. "Okay," Mirabel said to herself. She exhaled. "You got this."

The house quickly propelled her downstairs, past a portrait of Abuelo Pedro, whom she only knew through Abuela's stories. In the photo, he was young and very handsome. "Morning, Abuelo."

Mirabel began to set the table in the dining room. As she did, the house stirred, opening window shutters to let in golden rays of sunlight. Outside, a swarm of eager children from the village gathered at the window, anxious for tonight's big party. For them, the Madrigal family's gift ceremony was a huge event. The whole town looked forward to it and would come to celebrate.

As Mirabel prepared for breakfast, the children excitedly yelled questions from the window.

"Hey, when's the magic going to happen?!" a little boy shouted.

"My cousin's ceremony is tonight," Mirabel answered calmly, continuing to set up. It was important that she helped as much as she could. Today was a big day for her family.

"What's his gift?" yelled the same little boy, hoisting a cup of coffee.

"We're going to find out," Mirabel said.

"What's your gift?" another child asked.

"Who's asking?" Mirabel teased, not stopping her work for a second.

"Us!" said the little boy, gesturing to the three other children with him.

"Well, 'us,' if I only tell you my part, you won't know the whole story," Mirabel answered.

This time all the children chimed in. "What's the whole story?"

"Ah, you're not going to leave me alone, are you?" she said, returning to her bedroom. In order to tell children the whole story, Mirabel had to tell them all about her family and their magical gifts. And she would need a little help from Casita.

Casita was always there for Mirabel and the rest of the Madrigals. They shared a special bond, and each day was a new adventure at the magical house.

Ready to tell the story, Mirabel turned her attention to the drawers along the wall.

"Drawers," she said. They opened immediately for her. "Floors." The tiles on the ground flipped open and closed as if saluting her. "Doors." All the bedroom doors in the house glowed with magic.

"Let's go!" Mirabel shouted. Hurrying about, she and the house joined forces to wake up the rest of the family. Soon, every single member of the Madrigal family scurried to get dressed and grab a quick bite. Once the family was up and ready, everyone headed toward town to prepare for the special day. The children gathered at the front of the house to watch the magical Madrigals stroll by.

"Oh my gosh, it's them!" They squealed and pointed. "What are the gifts?! What does he do? What does she do?"

Mirabel smiled graciously. She supposed the kids had waited long enough. "All right, all right, relax," she said.

"It is physically impossible to relax!" screeched the little boy holding the cup of coffee. Mirabel eyed him with concern.

The rest of the children jumped in. "Tell us everything! Who can do what? What are their powers?"

The little boy with the coffee cup turned red

and shrieked louder. "Just tell us what everyone can do!"

"And that's why coffee's for grown-ups," Mirabel said, snatching away his cafécito.

As the children followed Mirabel through town, they passed a beautifully painted mural of Abuela with her triplets: Pepa, Bruno, and Julieta. Mirabel explained that they were the first to receive the magical gifts. Tía Pepa was given the power to control the weather with her moods. If she's happy, there's sunlight for days. If she's sad . . . better grab your umbrella! Tío Bruno has the power to tell the future. He mysteriously left the family long ago. And now the family doesn't talk about him. Next, Mirabel pointed out her mom, Julieta. She could heal any injury or illness with her food. As Mirabel and the children rushed by, her mom served arepas to a long line of people with various maladies.

All around Mirabel, the town buzzed with action and alegría. Children dressed in jerseys played soccer. On the other side of the street, a group ran a rowdy game of tejo. Every time a player struck the target with a rock, there was a loud *pop,* and everyone cheered. In the mercado, shoppers haggled with lively vendors for the best deal on hormigas Santandereanas and candles.

The children continued to follow Mirabel through town as she pointed out family members. Up next were her thoughtful father, Agustín, and the life of the party, Tío Felix. Neither man had any special magical powers, as they had married into the family. As for Abuela Alma, she was the most revered Madrigal of all! The entire village loved and respected her because she ensured that the family used their magical gifts for the good of the comunidad. As Abuela and the family hustled through town, helping people with a variety of tasks, the citizens called out to them with respect and adoration.

"Make way for the Madrigals!" a villager shouted.

"It's a big day!" another person exclaimed.

"Good luck tonight!" said another.

Mirabel paused to take a long look at her magical family. She yearned to make them proud.

"Wait!" one of the kids called out, watching the family walk by. "Who's a sister? Who's a cousin?!"

"How do you keep them all straight?" another kid asked in disbelief.

Mirabel faced the children with a flicker of amusement behind her oversize glasses. "Okay, okay, okay, okay . . ." As the children huddled closer, she identified her three cousins and two siblings and their magical gifts.

Cousin Dolores could hear a pin drop. You wouldn't want to whisper your secrets around her! Cousin Camilo was a shape-shifter, which was annoying when he shape-shifted into you! And Cousin Antonio, well, he didn't have a gift yet, but he would receive his today.

Mirabel pointed out her two older sisters: graceful Isabela and strong and responsible Luisa.

Isabela was Miss Perfect. She could make flowers bloom out of thin air with a flick of her dainty fingertips. Everyone adored Isabela, including the handsome Mariano, who was right at that very moment staring at Isabela with googly, lovey-dovey eyes.

Luisa was superstrong and responsible. Her biceps were as huge as her kind heart. Need a palm tree moved to provide better shade? No problemo! Luisa's got that! Is that church facing the wrong direction? Not a problem for Luisa! No request was ever too much for her.

Once Mirabel finished describing her sisters' and cousins' magical gifts, the bells of the town rang out. It was time for the family to go home. Abuela gave a satisfied grin at all the work that had been accomplished.

"Family, let's get ready!" she called out.

"Let's go, everybody!" Luisa yelled.

In a flash, the family gathered and headed home together. Mirabel hurried to follow them.

"But what's your gift?" a little girl asked, stopping Mirabel just as she was about to enter the house and escape their questions once and for all. Mirabel tried to stall and come up with a clever answer when Abuela Alma appeared at the doorway.

"What are you doing?" Abuela Alma snapped.

"Oh, uh," Mirabel stammered. "They were just asking about the family and—"

"She was about to tell us about her super-awesome gift!" one of the other little girls exclaimed. Abuela looked at Mirabel, confused.

"Oh, Mirabel didn't get one," Dolores answered, popping up from out of nowhere. Mirabel winced. She should have known that Dolores would hear that. Thinking she'd been helpful, Mirabel's cousin smiled and returned to whatever she'd been doing before. Mirabel peered over at Abuela Alma, who shook her head in disappointment and walked away.

The children stared at Mirabel like they'd been duped.

"You didn't get a gift?" the first little girl asked, looking up at Mirabel with sad eyes.

Mirabel was starting to spin an answer as a man and a donkey approached. "Uh—"

"Mirabel! Delivery!" the man called out. He quickly filled her arms with a basket of supplies for the ceremony. "I gave you the 'special' since you're the only Madrigal kid with no gift. I call it the 'not special' special. Since . . . uh, you have no gift."

Mirabel stood frozen. The children stared up at her. "Thank you," she said.

"And tell Antonio good luck!" the man replied, giving his donkey a pat. "Last gift ceremony was a bummer. The last one being yours that did not work." The man departed.

The kids were silent, staring hard at Mirabel. All she could do was stand there with a cheesy smile and her arms full of supplies.

"If I was you, I'd be really sad," said the little girl.

Mirabel forced a big smile and shrugged. "Well, my little friend, I am not, 'cause the truth is, gift or no gift, I am just as special as the rest of my family."

The children glanced over at her family performing amazing magical feats around the house and then back to Mirabel.

"Maybe your gift is being in denial."

# chapter TWO

In the courtyard, preparation for Antonio's gift ceremony was in full swing. No one even noticed Mirabel entering with her arms overflowing with groceries.

"Oh, sorry . . . excuse me . . . ," Mirabel said, struggling with the heavy load. The family chattered and talked over each other.

"Luisa, how are those pianos coming? Do you need help with that?" a voice called out.

"Lift it higher," another voice directed.

"Camilo," Abuela Alma yelled. "We need another José."

Mirabel's cousin Camilo yelled "Joooooosé!"

and changed into a tall guy. He helped hang a banner that said ANTONIO! over a door with a glowing border around it.

"Luisa, the piano goes upstairs," shouted Abuela.

"You got it," answered Luisa, hauling the piano over her shoulder.

As a swirling wind, caused by Tía Pepa, hovered over the courtyard, Mirabel tried to keep the load of supplies she was carrying from blowing away.

"My baby's night has to be perfect, and it's not perfect and—" Tía Pepa mumbled, pacing back and forth. Tío Felix rushed to calm her down.

"Amor, amor," he pleaded. "You're tornadoing the flowers," he said.

"Did someone say *flowers*?" said the sugary-sweet voice of Isabela, who was suddenly descending from the top floor on a flowery vine. A vibrant array of flowers bloomed, and petals fluttered everywhere.

"Our angel, our angel," Tío Felix praised.

"Please don't clap," Isabela implored them humbly.

"Ah, thank you," Tía Pepa said.

"Oh, it's nothing," Isabela answered. She landed gracefully in the courtyard next to Mirabel, who was now covered in petals. Mirabel quickly brushed petals off herself, hoping to look as elegant and graceful as her older sister.

"Relax. No one's looking at *you*," Isabela said.

"Well, they're only looking at you 'cause . . . you're so pretty," Mirabel responded. "Agh, Mirabel," she said to herself, wincing at the sloppy comeback.

Isabela glared at her as if saying "loser," then headed off in a different direction.

Determined to keep helping as much as she could, Mirabel hauled a heavy load of supplies onto the kitchen counter. Her mom noticed and sidled over.

"Whoa," her mom said with concern. "Mi vida, you okay? You don't have to overdo it."

"I know, Mamá. I just want to do my part like the rest of the family," Mirabel said, then let out a big grunt as she dumped another load onto the counter. The counter tiles quickly shuffled it away.

"She's right, amor," her father said, suddenly

in front of her with a swollen face covered in red welts.

"Eegh!" Mirabel winced. She glanced over to her mom. Her mom sighed and began pounding dough between her palms to make an arepa.

Her father continued. "First gift ceremony since yours, lot of emotions—"

"Bee stings," Mirabel announced to her mom.

"And . . . I've been there—"

"Ay, Agustín," Mirabel's mom said.

"When me and your tío Felix married into the family—outsiders who had no gift, never ever would, surrounded by the exceptional, it was easy to feel . . . 'un-ceptional'—"

"Okay, Papi," Mirabel said. Her father was insistent that she talk about her feelings on Antonio's special day.

"I'm saying I get it—"

"Eat," Mirabel's mom said, stuffing an arepa in Agustín's mouth, healing him instantly. She shoved him away and turned to Mirabel. "Mi amor, if you want to talk—"

"I gotta put out the stuff," Mirabel blurted, grabbing more supplies. "House isn't going to decorate itself." Suddenly, Mirabel realized what she had said. "I mean, you could," she said to Casita. "You look great." With her arms loaded, she headed out of the kitchen.

"Corazón, remember," Julieta called out after Mirabel, concerned. "You have nothing to prove."

"You have nothing to prove!" Mirabel's father bellowed. Satisfied with their little talk, he exchanged a "we nailed it" look with Julieta— but then a bee stung his nose, causing it to swell up again.

Later on, feeling great and *not* like she had anything to prove at all, Mirabel hauled a huge box to the second floor. She pulled out one candle after another and arranged them around the balcony. Throughout the house, there was busy chatter.

"Casita, the whole town is coming. The staircase should be twice as wide," someone ordered.

"Don't touch that! That's for Abuela," another voice said.

"Anybody seen my tiple?" someone else called out.

Mirabel felt disconnected from the planning

in the courtyard, but she was determined to find her own way to help on Antonio's special day. The box she was carrying had a special homemade gift for Abuela.

Mirabel moved down the hallway, still carrying the box, and paused briefly at the entrance of Tío Bruno's tower. His door was boarded up and covered with cobwebs. She looked at it with a mix of curiosity and fear. No one in the family talked about Bruno. What happened to him? Why did he leave?

Mirabel continued on. She knelt in the hallway and pulled out a beautiful candle doily she had made for Abuela. She gazed up at the wall above her. It was covered with photographs of her extraordinary family. As she looked over them, she realized her photo wasn't there.

*Of course it isn't,* Mirabel thought. This wall was for everyone who had received a magical gift. She knew she would never be on the wall with the rest of her family.

"One hour!" Abuela called out, startling Mirabel so much that she dropped a lit candle on the floor, setting the gift she had made for Abuela on fire.

Mirabel rushed to put the fire out, but the doily was destroyed. Suddenly, Abuela stood in front of her, watching the whole spectacle.

"Maybe you should leave the decorations to someone else?" Abuela said.

Mirabel, still on the floor trying to save the doily, glanced up at Abuela. "Oh, no, I actually made this as a surprise . . . for you."

Abuela looked down at Mirabel, not quite sure what to think. Then she noticed a dark cloud forming in the sky. She called to her daughter, "Pepa, the sky has a cloud."

"I know, Mamá, but now I can't find Antonio. What do you want from me?" Tía Pepa threw her hands up in helpless desperation, and the sky darkened. Abuela sighed, looked around, and checked her watch. People from the community would be here soon.

"I bet I can find him," Mirabel offered.

"Oh, I'm sure you need to go get cleaned up," Abuela said.

"It's no problem! Anything I can do to—"

"Mirabel," Abuela interrupted. "I know you want to help, but tonight must go perfectly. The whole town relies on our family, on our gifts. So the best way for some of us to help is to step aside, let the *rest* of the family do what *they* do best. Okay?"

"Yeah. Mm-hmm," she said with a nod.

Even though the words hurt her, Mirabel always went along with whatever Abuela asked of her. Mirabel loved her abuela and wanted to make her proud! She felt like she kept disappointing her. Abuela gave Mirabel a tight-lipped smile as a gust of wind gushed through the house.

"Pepa! Amor, the wind!" Abuela called out, rushing away.

"Ay! What do you want me to do? I need this muchachito," wailed Tía Pepa.

Mirabel went to her room, as her abuela had suggested. She knew how important tonight was to Abuela, to her family, and to the entire Encanto. Why couldn't Abuela see that she just wanted to make her family proud?

# chapter
# three

Mirabel sat at the edge of her bed and tried to shake off the conversation with her abuela. She glanced around the room; it was the same room every Madrigal child grew up in until they turned five. At five, she was supposed to have received her gift and new room, but she didn't.

Antonio's things were packed nicely and stacked on his bed, ready to be moved after the gift ceremony tonight. If all went as it should, he would have his own magical room and magical door. And Mirabel would be left behind once again. She straightened up. She knew what she had to do, and it didn't include sitting around feeling sorry for herself. Her little primo and soon-to-be former bedroom buddy needed her support.

She opened a drawer and pulled out a small wrapped package stenciled with designs that matched her dress. Mirabel put her fingers in the loop of the bow and dangled it over the edge of the bed.

"Everyone is looking for you," Mirabel said. There was no response. "This present will self-destruct if you don't take it in three, two, one. . . ."

Antonio's tiny hands popped out from under the bed and grabbed the present. Smiling, Mirabel scooched under the bed to join her small cousin hiding there.

"Nervous?" Mirabel asked. Antonio nodded. "You have nothing to worry about." Antonio nodded some more. "You're gonna get your gift and open that door, and it's going to be the coolest ever! I know it."

"What if it doesn't work?"

"Well, in that impossible scenario, you'd stay in here in the nursery with me. Forever. And I'd get you all to myself," Mirabel teased. Antonio looked over at her with a mix of regret and love in his eyes.

"I wish you could have a door," he said quietly. Mirabel's heart dropped. Antonio was a shy, quiet child who barely spoke, but he always felt comfortable enough to talk to Mirabel about how he felt. She loved him very much for all his shyness and thoughtfulness.

"You know what? You don't have to worry about me, because I have an amazing family and an amazing house and an amazing you," Mirabel said. "And seeing *you* get your special gift and your door, that's going to make me more happy than anything." Mirabel walked her fingers toward the present and pushed it closer to him. "But alas, I am going to miss having the world's best roomie."

She nodded to the present. Antonio opened it and pulled a hand-knit stuffed jaguar from the box. He immediately held it close. "I know you're an animal guy. And I made this so when you move into your cool new room, you always have something to snuggle with."

The house rattled the floorboards beneath them, reminding them it was time for the gift ceremony.

"All right, hombrecito, you ready?"

Antonio nodded. Mirabel moved to leave but turned back for one more cuddle with her little cousin.

"Sorry, gotta get one more squeeze," she said. The house playfully raised the floorboards, sending both of them tumbling out from under the bed. "Okay, okay! We're going! Ow!"

chapter
four

Throughout the town, excitement continued to grow. People celebrated with song, fireworks, and candles they carried as they made their way to the Casa Madrigal. It was a big night. It had been ten years since there was a gift ceremony, and the last one hadn't gone well. The entire town was hopeful for a successful night.

As the crowd arrived, every member of the Madrigal family had a role. Luisa took their guests' donkeys and hauled them to the appropriate area. At the front door, Camilo changed his size so he could look each person in the eye as he shook their hands and welcomed them. Once they were inside, the house took the people's jackets and hats as they moved toward the archway. Isabela showered each guest with flower petals. Unbeknownst to her, Mariano watched her adoringly. The townspeople gushed with amazement at the beautifully decorated magical house.

At the top of the stairs, Antonio's door glowed and sparkled. As children sprung up the stairs to see it closer, the stairs would transform into a slide, sending the thrilled children down to the first floor over and over again.

Mirabel walked Antonio to the foyer, where his ceremony would begin. As soon as his family caught sight of him, they rushed over.

"Papito! There you are. Ready for the big show?" Tío Felix asked.

"Look at you, all grown up," Tía Pepa said, tearing up and causing a storm cloud.

"Amor, you're going to get him all wet," Tío Felix said.

Camilo morphed into Tío Felix. "You make your papá proud," Camilo said, trying to impersonate his dad.

"I don't sound like that," Tío Felix complained.

"*'I don't sound like that,'*" Camilo mocked.

Dolores tilted her head as if hearing something from afar and then stepped forward. "Abuela says it's time."

Tía Pepa bent down to Antonio and kissed him. "Here we go, Tonito! We'll be waiting at your door!"

"Okay, vamos!" Tío Felix yelled excitedly.

"*'Okay, vamo—'*" Camilo, still disguised as his father, started to repeat before Tío Felix yanked him away.

Drums began to play. Abuela Alma entered the courtyard. Holding the magical candle, she addressed the crowd of family and townspeople.

"Fifty years ago, in our darkest moment, this candle blessed us with a miracle," Abuela said. "And the greatest honor of our family has been to use our blessings to serve this beloved community. Tonight, we come together once more as another steps into the light, to make us proud."

The crowd cheered, and a curtain opened to reveal Antonio, standing alone. He looked afraid to move. A hush fell over the house when Antonio didn't step forward. The house tried to encourage him, but he didn't budge. All eyes were on him as he stood frozen. He turned to Mirabel and held out his hand. Mirabel's heart sank. She knew Abuela would not approve. Plus, she couldn't help but think of her own gift ceremony. Her failure. What if that rubbed off on Antonio? She glanced over at Abuela holding the candle and then back to Antonio. She was torn on what to do.

"I can't . . . ," she whispered to him.

"I need you," Antonio whispered back.

Mirabel wondered if she should do it. Did she have the strength to step up and face the reminder of the worst night of her life? Did she have the courage to help her primito, knowing Abuela would not approve? Mirabel felt a glimmer of determination surge through her. If Antonio needed her, she was going to help him! She *was* going to walk him down the aisle so he could get his gift!

"Come on," Mirabel said to Antonio, taking his outstretched hand. "Let's get you to your door." Antonio held her hand tightly as they walked.

In the crowd, everyone panicked seeing Mirabel and Antonio. The last time she had made this journey, it was a failure for the familia.

With every step closer to the door, Mirabel felt the pain of her own failed gift ceremony. She thought back to the night: She reached out for the knob of a glowing door. Upon touching it, she was supposed to have been filled with magical light, but instead, the door's glow vanished! It left her without any special gift! From that point on, Abuela looked at her differently, and everyone's expectation of Mirabel changed. Mirabel looked at herself differently, too.

Doing her best to shove the painful memories away, she focused on walking Antonio toward his magic door. Once there, she handed him off to Abuela.

"Will you use your gift to serve this community?" Abuela asked Antonio. "Will you earn the miracle and make us proud?"

Antonio shyly nodded, and Abuela gestured for him to put his hand on the doorknob.

For a second, Mirabel saw worry in Antonio's

eyes, but when he touched the doorknob, his whole body lit up. He was filled with magic! Just then, a toucan landed on Antonio's arm. It chirped and flapped its wings.

Antonio's eyes widened, and he smiled. "Uh-huh, uh-huh, I can understand you," he said excitedly. "Of course they can come!"

Suddenly, dozens of animals flocked to him as his door transformed into a menagerie. Antonio could communicate with animals! Abuela was overjoyed that he had received his gift. She let out a huge sigh of relief and faced the guests.

"We have a new gift!" she announced. The crowd cheered, and more fireworks lit up the sky.

Antonio opened his door to find that his room was an enormous rainforest, full of animals and foliage. A jaguar scooped Antonio up onto its back and raced through the room as the boy laughed with delight.

"Wepa, Antonio!" cheered Tío Felix, watching his son and the jaguar whip around the rainforest. "Vaya, vaya!"

"You want to go where?" Antonio asked the

jaguar. The jaguar dashed up a tree trunk, tossing Antonio in the air. "Whoooooooaaa!" Antonio shouted with joy. He bounced across hammocks of coatis and skated on the surface of a river using a snake as a rope. He was having the time of his life!

After the wild ride, the jaguar and Antonio stopped in front of the family. While everyone celebrated, the jaguar playfully leapt on Agustín, knocking him over. Abuela pulled Antonio in for an embrace.

"I knew you could do it . . . a gift just as special as you!" she gushed.

Still at the threshold of the door, Mirabel stood back and watched her family celebrate. A mix of emotions took over. On one hand, she was so happy for Antonio, and on the other, she felt so alone and unworthy. She wondered if having a special gift was the only way to make her family proud. Was she even really a part of this family if she didn't have a special gift?

"We need a picture!" Abuela called out. "Family, come, come, come! It's a great night, a perfect night." The family quickly gathered close for a family picture. "Everyone say—"

"La Familia Madrigal!" the family shouted. No one noticed that Mirabel had not made it into the shot. She was on the outside corner. An outsider in her own family again. She walked away.

# chapter
# five

All day, Mirabel had put on a brave face, but now the hurt of being unseen and feeling unworthy rose like a looming shadow. She wanted more than anything to earn her spot in the family portrait. Everyone seemed to know their role and their place in the family. Was there still room on the wall for her?

Mirabel headed to the courtyard, leaving behind the dancing and music. She didn't feel like celebrating. Instead, she stared at the magical candle, hoping for another miracle. She wanted the candle to listen to her the way it had listened to Abuela so long ago.

Suddenly, there was a crackle. A tile from the rooftop came crashing down to the floor. Something was wrong. The house wouldn't just break like that! Mirabel quickly picked up the broken tile for closer inspection, cutting her hand on its sharp edges. She winced, briefly distracted by the pain. Then she noticed that all the courtyard tiles were fritzing out. They were malfunctioning! Mirabel watched them, confused. What was happening?

"Casita?" she said, her voice quavering. This had never happened before.

She placed her hand on the wall as if to comfort the house . . . when *CRACK!* A small fissure in the stucco began to form near her hand. The crack continued to spread along the wall; then it splintered. Mirabel stepped back, frightened. More cracks appeared, snaking across the wall. They rippled everywhere! Mirabel raced up the stairs to follow the main crack. It slithered past Abuelo Pedro's portrait and on to the second floor! For a second, Mirabel lost it, but then she heard the familiar chilling snap of the wall as it broke apart. She glanced down the hallway and saw the crack pass Isabela's room, nearly extinguishing the door's magical glow.

Mirabel continued to rush after it, following its trail past Luisa's door, then Bruno's creepy tower, on toward Abuela's door, and then to the candle! As the cracks swirled and multiplied, the candle's bright flame dimmed. Mirabel watched in horror as the whole house darkened around her!

Meanwhile, the celebration in Antonio's room was in full fiesta mode. On the dance floor, everyone twirled and stepped to the lively salsa music.

"Abuela!" Tío Felix exclaimed, pulling Abuela Alma up from her seat to dance. Abuela let loose with a few dance moves. "Okay, okay—wepa!"

Suddenly, Mirabel barged in, panicked. "The house is in danger! The house is in danger!" she screamed. The band stopped, and everyone gaped at Mirabel, concerned. "The tiles were falling, and there were cracks everywhere and . . . the candle almost went out!" Mirabel exclaimed, breathing hard. Everyone at the party began to murmur uncomfortably.

Abuela looked around, noticing how upset some

of the guests were. She needed to act quickly. She turned to Mirabel. "Show me."

Mirabel led the family to the courtyard, where the cracks had waged their destructive path, but when they arrived, there were no cracks in the walls! And the candle's flame shined brightly.

"It started right there," Mirabel said. "The house was breaking. The candle was in trouble. Casita?" Mirabel pleaded. The house didn't respond.

Abuela looked at the candle, then back to Mirabel, embarrassed and disappointed.

"Abuela, I promise, I—"

"That's enough," Abuela said, giving Mirabel a stern glance. The crowd exchanged nervous whispers. "There is nothing wrong with la Casa Madrigal!" Abuela said, turning to address the crowd with a confident smile. "The magic is strong . . . and so are the drinks! Please, music! Dance!"

Mirabel's father motioned to Luisa, who quickly brought him a piano to play to smooth over the awkwardness in the room. Isabela passed by Mirabel and scoffed at her. Again, Mirabel felt alone and confused. Around her, everyone headed back to the party, but not without first giving her a judgmental look.

Mirabel's mom glanced over at her with worry. Mirabel stood there, confused; she knew what she had seen.

# Chapter Six

As the party continued without her, Mirabel joined her mom in the kitchen. Mirabel was sure of what she had seen, even if the cracks were gone now. Surely her mom believed her.

"If it was all in my head, how did I cut my hand? I would never ruin Antonio's night. Is that really what you think?" Mirabel asked.

"What I think is that today was very hard for you."

"That's not . . . ," Mirabel started. "I was looking out for the family. And I might not be superstrong like Luisa or effortlessly perfect like

'Señorita Perfecta,' Isabela, who's never even had a bad hair day, but . . ." Mirabel sighed at how she sounded. "Whatever."

The house used the counter to deliver an arepa to Mirabel's mom.

"I wish you could see yourself the way I do," her mom said. "You are perfect just like this. You are just as special as anyone else in this family." Mirabel's mom pressed the arepa into her hand and held it tight.

"You just healed my hand with an arepa con queso."

"I healed your hand with my love for my daughter, with her wonderful brain . . . ," Mirabel's mom playfully responded, pulling her in for a squeeze.

Mirabel tried to wriggle away. "Ugh." She rolled her eyes.

"Big heart . . ."

"Stop."

"Cool glasses!"

"Mamá," Mirabel said as her mom gave her a big kiss on the cheek.

"Ay, te amo, cosa linda."

"I know what I saw," Mirabel said, not wanting to let the subject go. Her mom sighed.

"Mira, my brother, Bruno, lost his way in this family," Julieta said. "I don't want the same for you. Get some sleep. You'll feel better tomorrow."

Mirabel headed back to her room and sat on her bed. She couldn't help but think how pathetic her room was without Antonio. Now he had his own magnificent rainforest room, and she was left in the same boring place she had been her whole life. Unable to stop thinking about the cracks and the candle's dimming flame, Mirabel jumped out of bed and opened her door to get a peek at the candle. The cracks were nowhere to be found. In the quiet of the night, Mirabel heard a noise coming from Abuela's bedroom. Was she unable to sleep, too?

Mirabel tiptoed to her abuela's window and peered inside. Abuela was softly weeping! Alarmed, Mirabel stepped back. Abuela was the rock of the Madrigal family. What could possibly make her cry? Then Abuela pulled up the chatelaine that dangled from her waist. Among the many keys was a photo from her wedding day. With sadness in her eyes, Abuela gazed at her husband, Pedro.

"Ay, Pedro . . . what do I do? If anyone knew how vulnerable we truly we are . . . how quickly our home could be lost. Bruno knew the cracks would grow, that our magic might falter. And kept it from us. And now I need help, mi amor. Some way to keep our home from breaking. If the truth can be found, help me find it, help me protect our family, help me save our miracle."

Mirabel gasped. The cracks were real! The miracle was dying!

Mirabel hurried to the courtyard. She was shocked, but also determined—she knew what she needed to do.

Mirabel was going to find the answers. She would help Casita, her family, and Abuela.

"I will save the miracle," she said.

The house waved a window shutter excitedly, as if posing a question to her.

"Oh yeah. I have no idea how to save a miracle, but there is one person in this family who hears everything. . . ."

# chapter
# seven

The next morning, the sun rose over the Encanto and shined down on the patio, where the family was enjoying breakfast. Mirabel arrived, feeling determined. The house was in trouble and she had to do something to help, but she needed a little more information.

She gazed around and spotted Dolores in line, stacking her plate with food. With her superhuman hearing, Mirabel's cousin was the one person in the family who heard all the secrets around the Encanto. If something out of the ordinary had happened last night, Dolores would know.

"That's where I'll start," Mirabel whispered to herself. She rushed up to Dolores in the buffet line. "Dolores, hey," she greeted her. "You know, out of all my older cousins, you're like my favorite cousin. So I feel like I can talk to you about anything, and you can talk to me about anything, like the problem with the magic last night that no one seemed to know about, but maybe someone secretly knows about?"

"Camilo!" Tío Felix yelled. "Stop pretending you're Dolores so you can have seconds."

Suddenly, the Dolores in front of Mirabel morphed into Camilo. "Worth a shot," he said. The house took the food back and whacked his hands. "Ah! Ey!"

The real Dolores leaned in and whispered in Mirabel's ear. "The only one worried about the magic is you . . . and the rats, counting in the walls. . . ." There was a brief, awkward pause as Dolores thought about that. "And Luisa. I heard her sweating all night."

Mirabel lit up. That was something out of the ordinary! Luisa had to know something.

Mirabel spotted her sister flipping a table over for the family's breakfast. She was so strong that she could flip it with one hand.

"There we go," Luisa said with a satisfied grin. Mirabel was heading toward her when Abuela entered the patio.

"Everyone to the table," said Abuela. "Let's go, let's go."

Mirabel took Tía Pepa's seat next to Luisa.

"Luisa—"

"Family, we are all thankful for Antonio's wonderful new gift," Abuela said, interrupting Mirabel. Abuela went to sit in her chair, but a coati was in her seat.

"I told 'em to warm up your seat," said Antonio with a smile. It was one of the coatis from his new bedroom.

Abuela smiled back. "Thank you, Tonito. I'm sure today we'll find a way to put your blessing to good use." As Abuela sat down, the coatis picked her pockets. "We must never take our blessing for granted."

Mirabel homed in on Luisa. She was determined to talk to her sister about the magic malfunctioning the previous night. "Luisa, hey, do you maybe know some secret about the magic or something?" Luisa looked like she'd been caught. "You do!" Mirabel exclaimed, pounding the table.

"Mirabel," Abuela warned. "If you can't pay attention, I will help you," she said.

"I—I . . . ," Mirabel stammered.

"Casita," Abuela called out. And before Mirabel could even protest, the house moved her away from Luisa and next to Abuela. Abuela continued addressing the family. "As I was saying, we must work every day to earn our miracle, so today, we will work twice as hard."

There was a low grumble among the family.

"I'll help Luisa—" Mirabel blurted, and stood to return to her sister.

"Stop," Abuela said before continuing with her updates for the morning. "First, an announcement. I've spoken to the Guzmáns, and we'll be moving up Isabela's engagement to Mariano." Mirabel's eyes widened. "Dolores, do we have a new time?"

Dolores cocked her head a few times, as if

listening to something far away. "Tonight," she answered. "He wants five babies."

Isabela nervously sprouted flowers.

Abuela smiled wide. "Such a fine young man with our perfect Isabela will bring a new generation of gifts and hope to our Encanto. . . ."

Camilo morphed into Mariano and started making kissing noises.

Isabela swatted him with flowers to get him to stop.

"Okay, our community is counting on us. La Familia Madrigal!"

"La Familia Madrigal!" Everyone cheered.

Everyone got up from the table, and Mirabel turned back to Luisa. She was finally going to get her answers.

"Luisa, hey!" she said. But Luisa was already gone.

# chapter
# eight

When Mirabel finally caught up with her sister, Luisa was hauling a whole church on her back. As she put the church down, the priest blessed her. Luisa was barely done when other neighbors began to call out their requests.

"Luisa, can you reroute the river?" someone asked.

"Will do!" Luisa answered.

"Luisa, the donkeys got out again," another neighbor said.

"On it," Luisa responded. As she heaved a couple of donkeys over her shoulders, Mirabel approached her.

"Luisa, wait a second. Luisa—wait!"

But Luisa didn't wait. Instead, she moved faster. It was as if she was avoiding Mirabel. Mirabel moved quickly, determined to find out what her sister was hiding.

Mirabel finally caught up. "What's going on with the magic?"

"Magic's fine. I've just got a lot of chores, so maybe you should go home," Luisa said, dodging her question. She kept walking through the village with Mirabel close behind her.

A woman called out, "Luisa, my house is leaning to the—"

*Whack!* Luisa knocked the house straight and kept trudging along with the donkeys on her back.

"Luisa, you're lying," Mirabel pressed, running ahead of Luisa and cutting off her path. "Dolores said you were sweating all night, and you never sweat, so you must—"

"Hey, move. You're gonna make me drop a donkey." The donkeys' eyes widened with concern. Mirabel moved out of her way, and Luisa lumbered on.

"Luisa?! Will, you just—" Mirabel shouted after her big sister.

"Don't worry about it," Luisa said.

"Just tell me what you know. . . . Luisa? You're obviously nervous about something. Is it about last night? Luisa, if you know something, and you don't say, and it gets worse—"

Suddenly, Luisa stopped. She turned around to face Mirabel with an annoyed glare.

"I FELT SOMETHING!" Luisa yelled. The donkeys looked alarmed.

"Felt what?" Mirabel asked. "Something with the magic?"

"I didn't. On second thought, I didn't," Luisa sputtered. "There were no cracks. I'm good . . . everything's good. I'm not nervous."

Mirabel stared at her. What was going on? "Luisa?" Mirabel said gently.

"I'm NOT nervous," Luisa repeated.

"Okay . . . ," Mirabel said, unsure what was happening to her sister. Luisa was always the strongest, but now Mirabel could see that her big sister wasn't just carrying the donkeys, she was carrying a whole load of pressure and pretending it didn't exist. Why? For the familia?

Luisa put down the donkeys and told Mirabel the truth: She wasn't nervous, because she wasn't allowed to be nervous. She was expected to be the strong one in the family, to carry everything and never show when she was overwhelmed or scared.

For the first time, she opened up about all the work she felt obligated to do and the pressure she felt to meet every demand. If Abuela said that they needed to work doubly hard, that was what she was going to do.

After all, she had to earn the miracle! Make the family proud! Moving churches, crushing diamonds, and transporting donkeys were all part of a day's work for Luisa!

Luisa did everything without any hesitation or consideration of how hard or dangerous the work might be. But the pressure to do more and more was getting to be too much.

Once Luisa started to open up, she had so much to say. Like boulders rolling down a mountain, all of Luisa's emotions rolled out, unstoppable and mighty! Mirabel realized that her sister Luisa felt the weight of the world—no, the universe!—on her shoulders. She never said no to a request. She never took a break.

She was strong, but did that mean she didn't deserve some time for herself? Listening to Luisa, Mirabel finally understood the pressure her sister had been under all these years.

Then, not knowing what else to do, she gave her sister the biggest hug she could muster.

"I think you really need a break," Mirabel told Luisa. Luisa hugged her back . . . a little too hard. Mirabel tried to speak through the tight squeeze. "You deserve it."

"Luisa doesn't take breaks," Luisa answered, still smothering her in the hug.

"Suffocating!" Mirabel choked, tapping Luisa on the back. Luisa pulled back enough to look her in the eye. Mirabel could tell that her sister was debating whether or not to share something.

"You want to find the secret about the magic? Go to Bruno's tower, find his last vision."

"Vision? Vision of what?"

"No one knows. They never found it," Luisa said, setting Mirabel back down.

The two sisters stood in silence, understanding each other finally.

"Luisa! The donkeys!" yelled a townsperson, snapping Luisa and Mirabel out of their moment.

"Uh-huh, I'm on it!" Luisa pulled the donkeys up and over her wide shoulders.

Mirabel watched her with awe. "I'm serious about you taking a break—"

"You're a good one, sis! Maybe I will!" Luisa said, giving Mirabel's shoulder a light, friendly punch. Then she turned and headed toward town.

"Wait, how do you *find* a vision?! What does that even mean?!"

"If you find it, you'll know," Luisa yelled back as she headed over a hill. "But be careful. That place is off limits for a reason."

Mirabel turned back to the house and shuddered. There was no escaping her fate now. If she wanted answers, there was only one place she could get them: Bruno's tower.

# Chapter
# nine

Mirabel rushed back to the house. As she crossed the courtyard and headed to Tío Bruno's tower, she snuck past Abuela and Isabela talking, clutching her bag close.

"Yes . . . ," Abuela said.

"I can't think of a more perfect match," Isabela said.

"Such a respected . . ."

Mirabel glanced at Bruno's creepy door. Was she really doing this? She opened it and stood in the doorway, shocked by the dark and dusty room. Sand spilled from above, creating a curtain that blocked her view.

"Can you turn off the sand, Casita?" she called out. Nothing happened. It was like the house wasn't there. Mirabel looked toward the door, panicked. The floorboards outside the door fluttered and waved, but nothing moved inside of Bruno's room. "You can't help in here . . . ," Mirabel whispered.

Mirabel was really on her own. She had never been without Casita. The house fluttered its floors in the hallway again, this time to say it was worried for her.

She put on a brave face and casually waved its concern away. "I'll be fine," she said, looking at all the sand in front of her. "I need to do this. For you. For Abuela, and maybe a little for me." Mirabel took a few cautious steps deeper into the room. She spoke again, this time sounding almost as nervous as she felt. "Find the vision. Save the mir—*ack!*" Mirabel screeched as she fell through the sand!

She landed face-first on more sand and then slid down a giant dune. Once she came to a stop, she looked up to see that she was in a towering room. A large sand fall streamed over the tall walls. Her eyes caught sight of a sign that said VISIONS! with an arrow pointing up to the top of a rock mountain. From the top, a bright green glow radiated.

She had to get up there! Mirabel saw a long stairway. There must have been hundreds of stairs she would need to climb! *Great,* she thought. Without warning, Antonio's toucan landed next to her and smiled.

"Whoa. . . . Oh, hello," Mirabel said, greeting the bird. The toucan chirped back. "Lotta stairs. But at least I'll have a friend." The toucan looked at her, then flew to the top. "Nope, you flew away immediately."

She was on her own. "All right," she grunted, setting off from the bottom stair. One down, hundreds to go.

As she climbed higher and higher, each step was harder than the one before. Mirabel gritted her teeth and continued going up. In her exhaustion, she huffed out a little song.

"Welcome to the Family Madrigal. . . . Too

many stairs in the Family Madrigal. . . . You would think there'd be another way because we're magic, but no. . . . Magical how many stairs fit in here! *Who designed this?!*"

Finally, Mirabel arrived at the top of the stairs, only to find a large break in the path that would keep her from getting across and going any farther.

"Oh, come on!" Mirabel groaned, completely drained from her climb. The toucan swooped down next to her and perched on a railing made of rope. "We meet again. Don't suppose you can get me over there?" she asked the bird. The toucan hopped around on the little rope.

That was it!

Mirabel knew what she had to do! She quickly removed the rope and tossed one end around a tall boulder above her. "Okay, I can do this."

With the rope secured, she swung across the large gap between the stairs and the rest of the path. Stunned that she was able to make it to the other side, she started to celebrate—but the ledge cracked under her feet. She stepped away just before the ledge collapsed into the darkness. She and the toucan looked at each other in agreement—that was too close a call! She would have to watch her step in here.

Mirabel crept forward, entering the corridor of what appeared to be a forgotten temple. The large bird trailed her nervously. Everything about this place felt like a tomb. She looked around desperately for any sign of what she should do next. She didn't even know what she was looking for!

Soon, she spotted three panels with images. They showed some sort of magical process involving smoke and sand. As Mirabel studied the pictures, a pot near her feet moved. Mirabel yelped as rats—just as startled as she was—scurried away. They scampered behind a portrait of Tío Bruno. His eyes had been scratched out. Mirabel shuddered at the creepy image.

Another creak sounded, drawing Mirabel's eyes to a different room. The toucan took one look at what appeared to be the inner sanctum of Bruno's tower and flew off, spooked.

"Quitter," Mirabel quipped. She entered the dark room.

Inside, she found nothing except for a strange circle of sand on the floor in the center of the room. It was a dead end. Mirabel looked around, but there was no sign of anything. "Empty . . . ," she said to herself, stepping into the circle of sand.

As she entered the circle, an abrupt, harsh wind swept through the cavern, slamming the door shut and submerging Mirabel in pure darkness. She was starting to panic when, suddenly, she saw a glowing green light. The glow was coming from below. She was standing on it!

Mirabel began to dig in the sand, flinging it everywhere, to reach the bright green glow. She picked up a glimmering green shard. It looked like a piece of a broken emerald sculpture. There were more pieces just like it scattered all around her. This had to be one of Bruno's visions! It was exactly like Luisa had said—when Mirabel found pieces of a vision, she'd know what they were.

Just as Mirabel found the shards, the whole house shook. Abuela was sweeping the foyer when she noticed. She looked over at the candle. Its flame dimmed for a quick second.

Behind Bruno's door, Mirabel didn't notice the shaking. She was too preoccupied by the glowing green piece in her hand. She excitedly picked up another and studied it, turning it clockwise to reveal . . . her own worried face staring back at her.

"Me?" Mirabel gasped. Immediately, the ground under her rumbled. The entire cavern began to shake and break apart. Through the large gaps, sand poured into the room, covering the remaining shards. Mirabel, in a last-ditch effort, dug for the remaining shard pieces and quickly put them in her bag. As pieces of stone and sand threatened to block the entrance and trap her inside the cavern, Mirabel saw the glow of one final piece she'd missed. She dived and grabbed it, but now the closed door wouldn't open. Mirabel banged at it desperately. She threw her body against it, but it didn't budge.

Then she had an idea! She jiggled the handle. It opened!

*Whoosh!* A tidal wave of sand pushed her out of the room.

Safe and sound, she gazed down at the shard with her image. Was Tío Bruno's very last vision about her?

# chapter
# ten

Mirabel raced out of the room, turning the corner so fast that she slammed right into Abuela. She lost grip of her bag, and all the vision shards she'd collected spilled out onto the floor.

"Where are you coming from in such a hurry?" Abuela asked.

"Uh, I'm sorry. . . . I was, um . . . ," Mirabel stammered nervously, trying to pick up the shards as fast as she could without drawing Abuela's suspicion. It was no use. Abuela always suspected Mirabel of something. Abuela began to look down at the shards on the floor, when a loud cry distracted her.

"My gift!" Luisa wailed, staggering up the stairs. "I'm losing my gift!"

"What?" Abuela asked with alarm in her voice.

"I was supposed to be helping the town, and I took a break—not your fault," she said to Mirabel. "I knew it was wrong, and I fell asleep. And the donkeys were chomping on the corn, and when I tried to grab them, they were . . . heavy!" Luisa rushed off to her room, bawling. Mirabel stood there, mortified by what was happening to Luisa.

Abuela whipped around to face Mirabel. "Did you say something to her?"

"Uh . . . I just . . . ," Mirabel sputtered. The bells from the town rang out, snapping Abuela back to her tasks for the day. Mirabel let out a sigh of relief.

"The Guzmáns are expecting me," Abuela said. "Tell no one. There's nothing wrong with Luisa, and we can't have the family in a panic. Tonight is too important." Abuela rushed off.

Mirabel could hear Luisa sobbing behind her closed door. It flickered lightly as if its magic was fading.

Troubled by what was happening, Mirabel

went back to her room. She laid out the shards and tried to make sense of what they meant.

"Why am I in your vision, Bruno?" Mirabel asked out loud.

A flash of lightning and thunder shook the room. Startled, Mirabel turned to see Tía Pepa in her doorway.

"Tía, jeez!" Mirabel said.

"Sorry, I didn't mean to—" Tía Pepa said, trying to shoo the dark clouds away. "Shoo, shoo, shoo. I just wanted to get the last of Papito's things, and then I heard 'the name we do not speak.'" A rumble of thunder followed. "Great! Now I'm thundering. And that will lead to a drizzle, and a drizzle will lead to a sprinkle, and *phew. . . .*" Tía Pepa stopped and took a few deep breaths. "Clear skies, clear skies," she repeated to herself. As Tía Pepa struggled to calm herself and collect Antonio's clothes, Mirabel glanced at the shards. Tía Pepa was Bruno's sister. Surely she'd know something about what the visions meant.

"Tía Pepa," Mirabel began. "If *he* did have a vision about someone, what did it mean?"

"We don't talk about Bruno," Pepa answered.

"I know, it's just, hypothetically, if he saw you—"

"Mira, please. We need to get ready for the Guzmáns."

"Okay," Mirabel said, not ready to let it go. "But I just want to know if it was, like, generally positive or, like, less positive or—"

"It was a nightmare!" Tío Felix barged into the room, his usually cheery voice full of drama.

"Felix," Pepa said with a stern look at her husband.

"She needs to know, Pepi. She needs to know," pleaded Tío Felix.

"We don't talk about Bruno," Tía Pepa said.

"He would see something terrible, and then *crack, boom,* it would happen."

*"We don't talk about Bruno,"* Tía Pepa repeated. But Mirabel ignored her. She was grateful to receive some answers from Tío Felix. Finally, someone was talking about Bruno.

"What if you didn't understand what he saw?" Mirabel asked.

"Then you'd better figure it out, because it was coming for you!"

Tía Pepa moved closer to her husband, hoping to stop him from talking about Bruno any further. Tío Felix gave her a look that urged her to spill the truth. It was time.

Hesitantly, Tía Pepa recalled their wedding day. There hadn't been a cloud in the sky until Bruno appeared. He'd arrived and told them it looked like it was going to rain. They ended up getting married in a hurricane. As they described the day, Mirabel could practically feel the heavy winds whooshing and the raindrops swooshing across her face.

As Pepa and Felix went on about their wedding day disaster, other members of the family appeared at the door. Cousin Dolores pulled Mirabel to the side to share her own experiences with Bruno. She explained that she had grown to live in fear of Tío Bruno. He was always muttering and mumbling to himself, and she could hear it all with her superhuman hearing. She even came to associate the sound of falling sand with him. Mirabel's eyes went wide as she remembered all the sand in Bruno's tower. Could Dolores hear the sand from all the way out here?

For Camilo, Tío Bruno was a larger-than-life monster who prowled around the town dressed in black, feasting on people's dreams! Mirabel was finally starting to understand why no one talked about Bruno. Every story was horrific— all except one.

It was Isabela's.

Of course, Isabela boasted that Bruno had predicted that she'd have all she desired in life! How much more perfect could you get?

Dolores sidled up to Mirabel again and added that Bruno had told her that the love of her life would marry another. What awful luck! No wonder her family never mentioned him.

As the family finished their nightmare stories about Bruno, Mirabel wondered if it would be better if she heeded Tía Pepa's warning and didn't mention Bruno ever again. After all, he had left the family.

The Madrigals had other things to worry about tonight. The Guzmáns were on their way. Mariano Guzmán was coming to propose to Isabela!

As the family rushed off to get ready for the

Guzmáns' visit, Mirabel checked on Luisa. She was shocked to see that her sister was having trouble opening an ordinary pickle jar.

Mirabel backed away. But when she passed by Luisa's door, its glow flickered and dimmed. Was Luisa right? Was her magic fading? Maybe there were still a few things to worry about in addition to the Guzmáns.

Mirabel had no time to waste. She ran back to her room to study the vision. It showed her standing in front of the cracked casa.

"Miraboo!" Mirabel's father called out to her. He poked his head into the bedroom and broke her train of thought. "Got your party pants on? 'Cause I do—"

His eyes narrowed in on the vision. He looked at Mirabel, alarmed. The house tried to hide the vision behind Mirabel but did a poor job of it and was much too slow. He'd seen it. Mirabel was busted! For a second, she considered making up a story, but she couldn't think of one. She came clean.

"I broke into Bruno's tower; I found his latest vision. The family's in trouble, the magic is dying, the house will fall. Luisa's gift is gone, and I think it's all because of me," Mirabel blurted.

Her father stood in silence.

"Pa?"

His eyes widened as if he was formulating a plan.

Before Mirabel knew it, he started shoving the shards into his pocket and rambling.

"We say nothing. Abuela wants tonight to be perfect until the Guzmáns leave. You did not break into Bruno's tower. The magic is not dying. The house will not fall. Luisa's gift is not gone. No one will know. Just act normal. No one has to know."

Suddenly, there was a noise outside the door. Dolores stood across the courtyard on the other side of the balcony, staring back at them with wild and worried eyes. She'd heard everything! Agustín and Mirabel were both busted!

# Chapter
# Eleven

In the large dining room, the family sat around a big table set with the best silverware and dishes. Next to Abuela were their special guests of honor: the handsome Mariano Guzmán and his abuela, who had a reputation for being very proper. Abuela Alma placed the magical candle nearby to impress them. She believed that a match between Mariano and Isabela was a major win for the family and the whole community.

Mirabel took her seat at the table between Isabela and her father. Knowing that tonight was an important dinner, *and* that Dolores knew about the vision, Mirabel did her best to act as normal as possible. However, she didn't trust Dolores *not* to tell everyone what she'd heard. Sitting across the table from her cousin, Mirabel watched Dolores with unwavering eye contact.

Dolores glanced at Luisa, who could barely lift her plate, and then back at Mirabel. Mirabel pressed forward with intense eyes that said, "Don't you dare!" Dolores stared back, pained. She was struggling to hold the secret. Mirabel shot Dolores a stern look. Tonight was not the time for it! Dolores glared back, looking like she'd pop at any second!

"No, it is we who are honored to dine with la Familia Madrigal!" Abuela Guzmán exclaimed. "Such a reputation, though when it comes to Mariano, it is always best to see for yourself."

Abuela Alma raised her glass, and everyone followed suit. "Yes, well then, to a perfect night!" she toasted with a slightly nervous smile.

"To a perfect night. Salud!" everyone replied.

As the two abuelas continued to chat, Mirabel held Dolores's gaze with a silent warning: do not say anything!

"Potatoes?" Mariano passed a bowl to Mirabel, forcing her to break her gaze with Dolores. As soon as Mirabel's eyes were off her, Dolores leaned over to Camilo and whispered in his ear. Camilo immediately started choking on his food. His head morphed into Abuela Guzmán's head, and food flew out onto the table in front of him.

"Camilo, fix your face," Tío Felix said. Camilo's face turned back to his own, and he glanced at Luisa and then back to Mirabel. She gave him the same intense stare of silence that she'd given Dolores.

"Water?" Isabela said. The jug of water passed by, blocking Mirabel's view. Once out of her sight, Camilo was telling his dad.

Tío Felix's eyes widened. He began choking on a bit of food, which he coughed up onto Abuela Guzmán's plate!

The whole table froze. What was happening? Abuela Alma, alarmed by everything she'd seen, tried to carry on as normal. "Casita! I think we need a new plate," she ordered.

The house fritzed and tried to deliver a plate, but instead, it fumbled several plates, which fell to the floor with a loud *clang* that spooked some of Tonito's animal friends.

Abuela Guzmán looked weirded out but pretended not to notice any of the strange behavior around her. "The entire Encanto was so relieved Antonio received his gift. Nice to know the magic is stronger than ever," she said.

Luisa struggled to hold in a sob.

"Yes . . . very true, very true," Abuela Alma said, smiling. "Mirabel? The salt, please?"

Happy to be helpful, Mirabel smiled at her abuela and turned to her father, seated next to her, for the salt. "Papá? The salt?"

Mirabel's father tried to hand her the salt, but his hand shook uncontrollably. Mirabel quickly took it and passed it to Abuela.

"Gracias, Mirabel."

"No problem, Abuelita." Mirabel smiled wide. "All I want to do is *help* this family."

Thunder rumbled.

Pepa!

Tío Felix had just finished whispering in Pepa's ear, and now a small swirling hurricane formed over the dining room table.

"Ah, how curious," Abuela Guzmán said, noticing the small storm.

"Pepa? The cloud," Abuela said, embarrassed.

Julieta leaned over to her sister, concerned. Pepa then whispered in *her* ear, causing Mirabel's mom to flush.

"What?" Julieta asked with alarm. She looked to Mirabel, deeply worried. Trying to avoid her mom's gaze, Mirabel glanced down at the floor . . . where tiny cracks formed. She dropped lower under the table to get a better look. They were spreading everywhere!

"Mirabel," Mariano called out. Mirabel sat up fast and bonked her head on the table. "Any more cracks? Or do you only see 'em when you're trying to get me off the dance floor?" he said jokingly. He chuckled in his light, charming way, not realizing cracks were forming under all of them! The two abuelas laughed politely, but Mirabel could see that her abuela was sweating.

"Ha! Yes. No—that's a very humorous question," Mirabel answered, stealing a glimpse at the cracks' progression across the floor. Soon, Antonio's animals started fluttering and making a nervous commotion when they saw the cracks, too. "And speaking of questions—popping questions—was there any . . . uh, *question* you wanted to ask Isabela? Tonight? Like now, like right now?"

Isabela turned to Mirabel, annoyed.

Confused by the sudden turn of events, Abuela Guzmán spoke up. "Well, since everyone here has a talent, my Mariano wanted to begin the night with a song. Luisa, could you bring the piano?"

Luisa, who was crying at the far end of the table, lifted her head.

"Okay," she sobbed. She got up slowly from the table and slogged away to get the piano that she knew she couldn't lift.

The cracks multiplied. There was definitely no time for a romantic song. The family was in danger. The proposal had to happen now so the Guzmáns could leave. Mirabel rose from her seat.

"It's actually family tradition to sing *after*," Mirabel said, shoving Mariano down on one knee in front of Isabela. She motioned for him to begin.

"Uh . . . Isabela, most graceful of the Madrigals . . . ," he stammered.

As the cracks continued to spread under the length of the table, Mirabel tried to shield the family from seeing them by awkwardly moving too close to Mariano and Isabela. In her peripheral vision, she noticed Tía Pepa squinting at something on the wall. Did she see the cracks, too? Thunder exploded above them.

More thunder erupted, frightening the animals, who quickly scurried under Agustín's chair. Some of the coatis spotted the glowing shards in his pocket. Noisily, they started tugging them out and assembling them on the floor.

"The most perfect flower in this entire . . . Encanto . . . ," Mariano continued, trying to get through the proposal, despite the sudden change of weather and the loud scraping noise on the ground as Luisa dragged the piano. "Will you . . ."

Abuela Guzmán watched in confusion. Then, just as Mirabel shifted a bit, she saw the cracks snaking through the house. "What is happening?!" Abuela Guzmán screamed.

Abuela Alma was absolutely mortified. This evening had gone horribly wrong! She knew she could no longer hide the truth. Just as she was about to speak, Dolores jumped in.

"Mirabel found Bruno's vision: she's in it, she's gonna destroy the magic, and now we're all doomed!" she blurted.

As if on cue, the clever coatis took the vision from the floor to the table for everyone to see. There was no denying it! Fully assembled, the vision showed Mirabel in front of a cracked Casita. Everyone gasped and looked back and forth from Mirabel to the vision.

Then the cracks rippled through the rest of the house, seemingly from where Mirabel stood. Everyone's powers were on the fritz! The house freaked out and knocked over chairs. The piano tipped over. And above, a storm cloud unleashed a torrent of water onto the table. In shock, Isabela blasted a bunch of flowers straight onto Mariano's face!

"Ah, my nose!" he screeched. "She broke my nose!"

Even worse, the candle's vase was cracked, too. The magic candle was melting! The whole family turned to Mirabel with accusatory looks as if it was all her fault. In their view, the vision pointed at her as the one to blame for all the destruction. Even her mom seemed convinced it was Mirabel's fault.

"Abuela . . . I . . . ," Mirabel stammered.

"Come, Mariano!" Abuela Guzmán ordered. "I've seen enough! We're leaving!" She got up and marched out of the dining room toward the courtyard, careful to dodge animals on her way out.

"Wait! Señora, por favor!" Abuela pleaded, getting up to follow her and Mariano.

"Abuela, please!" Mirabel said.

Abuela whipped around. "Stay right there! Not another word! Go to your room!" she ordered Mirabel.

"It's not my fault!"

Isabela stomped past Mirabel. "I hate you!" she shouted, running upstairs to her room.

Luisa passed Mirabel without a word, bawling. "Ahh, I'm a loser!"

"Luisa!" Agustín called out, scurrying up after her.

"What did you do?" Julieta said to Mirabel, chasing after Isabela. "Isa! Wait!"

More cracks rippled through the house.

"I'm not doing anything! It's not me, it's Bruno!" Mirabel yelled to anyone who would listen.

"Bruno isn't here!" Abuela snapped.

Suddenly, a green glow gliding along the ground caught Mirabel's eye. It was a part of the vision, but how was it moving?

"I know that . . . ," Mirabel said, transfixed by the moving green shards. She watched them until she saw that it was rats transporting the pieces! "I know he isn't . . . here."

Rats were taking the vision from the dining room up to the second floor.

"We are fine!" Abuela shouted to the Guzmáns. "The magic is strong!" She slammed the door shut behind them. "We are the Madrigals!"

Then she turned and shouted, "Mirabel!"

But Mirabel was gone.

Chapter
twelve

Thunder rumbled and lightning flashed throughout the Encanto.

Mirabel followed the rats. They would lead her to answers. She just knew it! She pursued them along the upper walkway of the house. She was closing in when, after turning a corner, they vanished.

Mirabel looked around for any sign of them. She heard a noise and caught a glimpse of a single rat tail disappearing through an opening under a large painting. Mirabel cautiously approached it. She studied the frame and then slowly pulled it open like a door, revealing a secret passageway within the walls of their house.

She stepped though the passageway to find that although it was murky, she could see the walls were covered in creepy cracks. They seemed to move across the walls, undulating as if alive.

A rat carrying a vision shard scurried past Mirabel's feet and into the darkness. She watched the green glow retreat into the empty space and then float up as if someone was lifting it. Mirabel squinted to get a better look at a form taking shape in the green glow of the shard.

*Crack!* A bolt of lightning lit the room and revealed . . . BRUNO! He held a rat in his hand and took the shard from it.

Mirabel and Bruno stared at each other for a second, and then in another *crack,* he was gone! His shadow streaked down a corridor.

She couldn't let him go. This was her only chance to learn the truth about the vision. She raced after him.

"Stop!" she shouted, running down the winding corridor, keeping up with every tight corner and unexpected drop.

Meanwhile, on the other side of the passageway wall, in Tía Pepa's room, Camilo tried to calm his mom, who was still shaken by the revelation that the family's magic was dying.

"It's okay, Mami. Deep breath in, deep breath out . . ."

Mirabel ran hard into the wall, causing Pepa to jump at the impact and zap Camilo with a bolt of lightning.

As Mirabel recovered from the collision with the wall, she closed in on Bruno.

"Stop! Stop!" she shouted.

Suddenly, he jumped a chasm in their path. Mirabel stopped, unsure that she could make the leap across. It looked very deep and very wide. Bruno ran ahead. He was getting away!

Mirabel summoned all her courage and leaped. She made it, but as soon as she landed, the ground crumbled under her. She barely caught the edge, but her fingers were slipping and losing their grip. She looked down at a deep, endless pit of darkness.

"No, no! Help!" she cried. "Casita?! Casita?! Help! Help me!"

Her fingers could no longer hold on, and she began to fall. Suddenly, her hand was grabbed in midair by . . . Bruno. He pulled Mirabel up onto her feet.

She was now face to face with her infamous tío Bruno. At first glance, he appeared sinister and ominous, but as a light fell across his face, Mirabel saw that he wasn't at all what she had imagined or what she'd been told. He was thin and lanky, but he also looked like he belonged to her family. He looked like a Madrigal. He was one of them.

"You are very sweaty," he said to Mirabel. Mirabel was shocked by his soft voice, but before she could respond, the floor beneath Bruno collapsed.

"Oh no!" Mirabel exclaimed.

He fell through, plummeting to . . . the floor just a few feet beneath them both. Bruno looked around, shocked to be standing. "Huh," he said. Then he took a long look at Mirabel. "Bye." He turned and walked away.

# Chapter
# thirteen

"What? No—hold on!" Mirabel hurried after him. She followed him through the back of the house, where they were surrounded by pipes, old furniture, and relics. As Mirabel struggled to keep up with him, she noticed that he behaved in an extremely superstitious manner. Bruno avoided stepping on any cracks. He tossed salt over his shoulder. And he made repetitive actions, all to avoid some unknown disaster.

But Mirabel had more important things to ask her long-lost uncle about.

"Wait, why was I in your vision? What does it

mean?" Mirabel asked as Bruno kept moving. "Is it why you came back?"

Bruno stopped and tapped a wall. "Uno, dos, tres, four, five, six." He held his breath.

Mirabel watched him curiously.

"Tío Bruno?" Mirabel said. He walked past a set of pipes and exhaled.

"Uno, dos, tres, four, five, six. You were never supposed to see the vision, no one was. . . . Little salt." He threw salt behind his back, hitting Mirabel.

"But . . . ," Mirabel sputtered, spitting out salt.

Bruno whistled. "My three whistles . . . spin around. . . . Aw, that feels better, that's better . . . ," he mumbled to himself.

Mirabel continued to follow him. She needed answers. They passed an area with tons of cracks that had been patched up. Mirabel's eyes widened in awe at the work. "Wait, have you been in here patching the cracks?"

Bruno stopped and took a long look at all the patch work. "Oh that? No, no, I'm too scared to go near those things," Bruno answered. "All the patching is done by Hernando."

"Who is . . . Hernando?"

Tío Bruno pulled on his hood. "I am Hernando, and I am scared of nothing," he said in a low voice. Then he removed the hood. "It's actually me," he said using his normal voice. Then he plopped a bucket over his head. "I am Jorge. I make the spackle."

Mirabel stared at him, realizing that Tío Bruno might have completely lost his mind.

"How long have you been back?" she asked gently. Bruno looked at Mirabel and then at the rat on his shoulder, as if debating with it about how to answer. Mirabel looked around and noticed the weird odds and ends of a home here behind the walls. There were knickknacks and family heirlooms. It hit Mirabel like a bolt of lightning.

"You never left," she blurted.

"Well, I left my tower, which was, you know, a lotta stairs, and, uh, in here I'm kitchen adjacent, plus free entertainment." Bruno motioned to a makeshift rat theater he had made with cardboard cutouts that the rats poked their faces through to get to the food on the other side. Unknowingly, they performed little plays. "What do you like?

Sports? Game show? Ooh, telenovelas? The love that could never be," Bruno rattled on.

"I don't understand."

Bruno gestured to his homemade rat theater.

"Well, see, what happened is, she's his aunt but she has amnesia, so she can't remember that she's his aunt. It's like a very forbidden kind of—"

Mirabel pushed away the cardboard theater to get Bruno to focus.

"I don't understand why you 'left' but didn't leave?"

Bruno looked down and shifted uncomfortably. "Oh, well . . . the mountains around the Encanto are pretty tall . . . and like I said, free food . . . and, uh . . ."

Mirabel saw a shaft of light coming through the wall. She followed it and peered through to discover the Madrigal family dining room on the other side. On his side, Bruno had placed a lonely table and chair for one. Mirabel's heart dropped. She looked up at him with the sad realization that it was his way of still being part of the family dinner. He had never wanted to leave them— something pushed him out.

# ❦ Meet the Madrigals! ❦

## Casita

Casita is the magical house where the Madrigal family lives. It is a miracle hidden in the mountains of Colombia in a charmed place called the Encanto. Like a member of the family, Casita is always there to assist, whether it's helping set up the dinner table, moving a staircase, or simply waving a window shutter to say hello!

## Mirabel

Mirabel is the only member of the Madrigal family without a magical gift. Bright and funny, Mirabel is always looking for ways to prove herself and express her love for her big, wonderful family.

## Abuela Alma

Abuela Alma is the matriarch of the Madrigal family. The magic of the Encanto blessed her family with magical gifts. She loves her family deeply and always wants what's best for them.

# Antonio

Quiet and kind, Antonio was on the shier side until he received his magical gift on his fifth birthday. He has the ability to communicate with animals, and his bedroom is a beautiful rainforest.

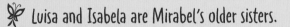
❀ Luisa and Isabela are Mirabel's older sisters.

## Luisa

Luisa is superstrong and the rock of her family. Whether it's rerouting a river or moving a whole church, Luisa is ready to lend a hand.

## Isabela

Isabela makes beautiful flowers wherever she goes. Graceful and poised, she seems perfect in every way and gets along with everyone—except for Mirabel.

## Julieta

Julieta has the power to heal physical injuries through foods like arepas con queso. She is warm and kind, especially when Mirabel feels left out because she doesn't have a magical gift.

## Agustín

Agustín married into the Madrigal family and has no magical powers of his own. He is thoughtful and supportive, always there for his family despite being accident-prone.

## Pepa

Pepa was gifted the ability to alter the weather with her emotions. When she is worried, she conjures a small tornado that whips through the Encanto.

## Felix

Felix is a devoted husband and father. Like Agustín, he has no powers and married into the Madrigal family. His outgoing nature makes him the life of every party at Casita.

## Dolores

Dolores has superhuman hearing and always knows what's happening around the Encanto. It's impossible to keep a secret from her!

## Camilo

Camilo can shape-shift. He often transforms into other people to help out around Casita and the rest of the Encanto.

# Bruno

Bruno has the ability to see the future. He left the family after Mirabel didn't get a magical gift. His visions scared people, and the family believed he made bad things happen. Now they refuse to talk about him.

Bruno looked away, embarrassed. "My gift wasn't helping the family," he said sadly. "But I love my family. I just don't know how to . . . how to, you know." He met Mirabel's gaze. It dawned on her that both of them were so alike in so many ways. She loved her family, too, but often felt unseen and unworthy. Bruno shook off the sadness. "Anyway, I think you should go, because . . . well, actually, I don't have a good reason. I'm just getting uncomfortable."

Mirabel moved closer to Bruno to really look at him. Her eyes were opened; now she knew that he had never meant any harm to the family. All those stories that her family had told—they simply didn't see what she could. She pressed on.

"Why was I in your vision? Tío Bruno?" He gave her a look that suggested he doubted she would understand, but she knew exactly how he felt. She didn't have a gift like he did, but somehow, she was hurting the family and not helping. Maybe the vision had the answers. "I just wanted to make the family proud of me. Just once," Mirabel said softly. "But if I should stop . . . if I'm hurting our family? Just tell me."

Bruno looked at her. He wasn't sure if he should reveal his deep secret. "I can't tell you—"

Mirabel let out a frustrated sigh and looked away.

"Because I don't know." Bruno grabbed the shards from his pocket and assembled them. "I had this vision the night you didn't get your gift," he explained. "Abuela worried about the magic, so she begged me to look into the future, see what it meant." As he talked, Bruno drifted back to that fateful night. His memories played out in the glowing green shards. "And I saw our house breaking, the magic in danger, and then I saw you. But the vision was different, and it would change. And there was no *one* answer. No clear fate. Like your future was undecided, but I knew how it was gonna look. I knew how it was gonna look because I'm Bruno and everyone would assume the worst, so . . ."

Mirabel now realized it was Bruno who had smashed the vision. He didn't want anyone to see it and possibly use it against her. He'd been doing her a favor.

"I don't know how things will go, but my

guess—whatever's happening, the cracks, the magic, the fate of our entire family . . . it's gonna come down to you."

"Me?" Mirabel said with wonder. Maybe the vision didn't mean she'd destroy the house and the magic. Maybe it meant she'd *save* it!

"Yeah," Bruno said, then he looked up at her with a shrug. "But you dug up the vision and showed the family anyway, so who knows, maybe you *do* wreck everything."

Mirabel's face dropped as her hope crumbled.

Bruno grabbed a cup of coffee, pulled a rat out of it, and drank from it. "Or you don't. It's a mystery, that's why my visions are *pfffpffftttt!*" He made a raspberry noise.

Tío Bruno put an arm around her shoulders and walked her to a door. "Look, if I could help any more, I would, but, uh . . . what's next is up to you." He ushered Mirabel out into the empty space between the walls of her house and shut the door behind her.

Mirabel stood stunned. Tío Bruno had said the vision was unreadable. He said it would constantly change. Everything undecided. No clear fate. Mirabel thought long and hard about this, but then through the walls, she heard her family's anguished voices.

"It was supposed to be perfect. I hate her!" Isabela cried.

"Luisa's a mess! Her gift is completely gone!" Julieta exclaimed.

"How do we even know the Encanto is still safe?" Tío Felix asked.

"Is she gonna make me lose my magic?" Camilo whined.

"Mirabel was in that vision for a reason. What else could it mean?" Abuela Alma's voice bellowed over all the rest.

Mirabel wasn't ready to give up. So what if the whole family thought she was trying to destroy the magic? Their preoccupation with her was keeping them from seeing the whole picture! There was still a way to save the miracle and prove her worth to the family. An idea came to her. Determined, she stepped back through the door, and she wasn't going to let Bruno push her out this time!

# chapter
# fourteen

"You have to have another vision," Mirabel said, barging in on Bruno.

"What? No, no, I don't. I don't do visions anymore," he stammered, surprised by her quick return. He stumbled back from her.

"You can't say, 'The weight of the world is on your shoulders. The end,'" Mirabel pointed out. "If your fate's up to me, me says have another vision, maybe it'll show me what to do."

"No, I don't do visions anymore." Bruno shook his head vigorously.

"What is the harm in trying?" Mirabel urged.

"Look, even if I wanted to, which I don't," he

said, "you wrecked my vision cave—yeah, I know about that—which is a problem now because I need a big open space."

"Come on! The two family weirdos finding each other? Sounds like fate to me," Mirabel said, totally undeterred.

"I still don't have a big open space."

Suddenly, Antonio's toucan landed between them. Mirabel and Bruno turned around and saw an ancient tapir, a bored chigüiro, and the fierce jaguar, followed by Antonio.

"You could use my room. The rats told me everything," Antonio said, then shot a look at the jaguar. "Don't eat those." The jaguar, eyeing Bruno's rats, backed off.

Mirabel looked back at Bruno, unwilling to take no for an answer. "Tío Bruno, our family needs help," she said. "And you need to get out of here."

"You're not gonna leave me alone, are you?" Bruno replied.

Meanwhile, unbeknownst to Mirabel and the rest of her family, the candle flickered unnaturally on its special shelf in the courtyard. A group of children playing in front of the house watched in horror as a thin crack snaked across the ground next to them. The house shook, scaring the children away.

In the foyer, Abuela Alma called a family meeting. She homed in on Agustín. "You should have told me the second you saw the vision!"

"I was thinking of my daughter. Or does she not count?" Agustín shot back.

"Pepa, calm down!" Abuela exclaimed as sleet trickled on all of them.

"This is me being calm. I am calm!" Tía Pepa said.

"Mamá, you've always been too hard on Mirabel," Julieta said.

Just then, there was a crackling noise. New cracks streaked across the wall of the foyer, causing Abuelo Pedro's portrait to crash to the floor.

"Look around," Abuela said. "We must protect our family, our Encanto. We cannot lose our home."

Tío Felix appeared at the door. "Abuela, the town wants you. They're freaking out."

Abuela gazed toward the town. "When I come back, I will speak to Mirabel. Find her," Abuela ordered. The house trembled again.

## Chapter
# fifteen

Moments later, Mirabel and Bruno were in Antonio's rainforest room. Bruno got to work quickly, forming a circle for his vision. As he worked, all of Antonio's animals watched. The room rumbled and shook as if the house was suddenly unsteady.

"I think we need to hurry," Mirabel gasped.

"You can't hurry the future," Bruno said. Once Bruno finished his circle—passing over a stubborn chigüiro who was unwilling to move—he gave Mirabel a worried glance. "And what if I show you something even worse. If I see something bad, it will happen."

"I don't think you make bad things happen. I just think most people only see things a certain way," Mirabel answered. Bruno looked up at her thoughtfully. "You got this."

Antonio handed Bruno his stuffed jaguar that Mirabel had made for him. The thoughtful boy hoped it would make his uncle feel brave, just like it made him feel brave on his gift day. Bruno took the doll and held it close.

"For good luck," Antonio said. He sent a smile to Mirabel that said he believed in her; then he left them to their work.

Bruno glanced down at the stuffed jaguar he held in his hands. He exhaled and reached for his ruana. From the garment, he removed a gilded capsule. He opened the capsule and took a match from it.

"I can do this. I can do this. Uno, dos, tres, four, five, six." Bruno lit the match and ignited a pile of wet leaves. Very quickly, smoke spiraled around him and Mirabel. He closed his eyes and began to count. "Uno, dos, tres, four, five, six. . . . Uno, dos, tres, four, five, six." Magic filled the room.

Unbeknownst to Bruno, his door in the hall began to glow again. It had been years since Bruno's door had glowed; it had stopped the day he left the family.

Back in Antonio's rainforest room, *everything* was aglow! A wind kicked up, blowing leaves and turning the waterfalls into a mist that swirled around them. Mirabel glanced over at Bruno, whose eyes had turned bright emerald green and sparkled like glitter.

"You might want to hold on," Bruno warned. Mirabel latched on to his hand, squeezing tightly as the gust of wind and magic continued to swell until . . . *whoosh!* Mirabel was transported into the vision: In it, she saw her family being chased by an ominous crack! Then a shape emerged.

"I can't!" Bruno yelled in pain. "I can't! It's just the same thing!"

"No, I can't help if I can't see what to do," Mirabel said. "I need to know which way it goes— there's gotta be an answer we're not seeing!" All around them the rainforest shook. The magic was struggling.

"Tío Bruno, the family needs you," Mirabel

said, giving his hand a gentle squeeze to let him know that she believed in him. The encouragement worked. Tío Bruno's vision grew clearer and brighter. Mirabel could see something forming. What was it? She looked closer and saw a butterfly flitting toward a small glow.

"There! Over there!" she yelled excitedly.

"Butterfly. Follow the butterfly," Bruno said. "There's someone else. . . ."

"Who is it?" Mirabel looked closer, but the shape was still forming.

"Embrace her, and you will see the way. . . ."

"Who?" Mirabel asked.

"Embrace her. You will see the way. Embrace her, and you'll see the way," Bruno droned on, like a chant.

Mirabel stepped closer. She had to know who it was she was supposed to embrace. "Who—"

"Embrace her. You will see the way. Embrace her, and you'll see the way," Bruno repeated.

"Who is it?" Mirabel asked, stepping toward the figure to get a better look. Then it was clear. It was . . .

"Isabela!" Mirabel scoffed. A flash of light

ended the vision. Bruno shook himself back to the present.

"Your sister, that's great!" he said. But Bruno didn't understand. It wasn't great. Not after the disastrous proposal and all the other reasons Isabela disliked her.

Mirabel grabbed Bruno and headed for Isabela's room. Even though she knew Isabela was mad at her, there was no time to waste. The Encanto needed her.

# Chapter
# Sixteen

"What does that even mean? Is that a hug? Why would that make me 'see the way'? She won't hug me," Mirabel grumbled behind a potted plant in front of Isabela's door. "She hates me. Also, I ruined her proposal. Plus—"

"Mirabel," Bruno said calmly behind another tall potted plant.

"It's just annoying. *Of course* it's Isabela."

"Mirabel."

"Señorita Perfecta always has to have all the answers."

"Mirabel." Bruno spoke a little louder to get Mirabel's attention. "Sorry, um, you're . . . you're missing the point. The fate of the family is not up to her, it's up to *you*," he explained. "And before you say you can't get a hug, you helped Antonio get his door, you helped me have my first good vision ever, you've never given up once. You're the best of us. You just have to see it." He smiled at her. "By yourself . . . after I leave."

"Wait, what? You're not coming?"

Bruno moved a potted plant and hid himself from view as he waddled toward the portrait that covered the secret passageway. Mirabel couldn't believe he was leaving her. "It was your vision, not mine!" he replied.

"You're afraid Abuela will see you," Mirabel said flatly.

"Yep! I mean, yes, that, too," he quipped. "If you save the magic, come visit."

"*When* I save the magic, I'm bringing you home," she said, smiling.

Bruno gave Mirabel a slight smile back. Then he picked up a rat from the ground and started talking to it. "Uno, dos, tres, four, five, six." He inhaled a large breath and then disappeared behind the portrait, into his secret passageway.

Mirabel was suddenly overcome with sadness. She looked toward the candle. Its flame was almost gone. The house flickered and fritzed.

Mirabel was running out of time. She opened Isabela's door and entered a gloriously flower-laden room. Everywhere Mirabel looked, there were vibrant flowers and lush green vines, but Isabela was nowhere to be found.

"Hi, sister!" Mirabel said in the sweetest voice she could muster. "I know we had our issues, but I'm . . . ready to be a better sister. So we should just . . . hug it out."

"Hug it out?" Isabela's voice snapped from out of nowhere. Mirabel winced. This was going to be tougher that she expected. "Luisa can't lift an empanada. Mariano's nose looks like a smashed papaya. Have you lost your mind?"

Mirabel searched the room for Isabela, finally spotting her lying on her bed, surrounded by even bigger and more over-the-top flowers than usual. "Isa, I know you're upset . . . and you know what cures being upset? A warm embrace."

"Get out."

A flowery vine wrapped around Mirabel and began to pull her out of the room.

"Isa—" Mirabel was beginning to protest when a flower jutted from the vine and covered her mouth.

Isabela took this opportunity to tell Mirabel how she really felt.

"Everything was perfect! Abuela was happy. The family was happy. You want to make things better? Apologize for ruining my life!"

Still wrapped in vines, Mirabel looked down, unsure of how to apologize for something that wasn't her fault. If anything, Isabela should apologize to her. The house shook again, and Mirabel knew she had to try. "I am . . . sorry . . . that your life is so great."

"Out!" Isabela fumed. With a wave of her hand, she made the plant drag Mirabel out the door, but Mirabel managed to grab a piece of furniture.

"Wait! Isa, fine," she said, surrendering. "I apologize. . . ." The vines gave her an extra tug. "I wasn't trying to ruin your life. Some of us have bigger problems, you stupid, selfish, entitled princess!"

"Selfish?!" Isa said with a scowl. "I've been stuck being perfect my entire life, and literally the only thing you've ever done for me is mess things up."

"Nothing is messed up! You can still marry that big, dumb hunk—"

*"I never wanted to marry him! I was doing it for the family!"* Isa shouted as a massive prickly cactus sprouted from the ground between the two sisters. It was strange-looking, unlike any cactus Mirabel had ever seen. More importantly, it was unlike any plant she had ever seen her sister make! It was far from the pretty flowers that decorated her room.

Isabela flinched, shocked by what she had created. Mirabel eyed the cactus, both freaked out and concerned.

"Isa?" Mirabel said softly. She glanced back at Isa's door. Its glow faded in and out wildly. Was this her fault? Had she just broken Isa's magic? "What is that?" Mirabel asked, uneasy.

Isabela stepped closer to the cactus, no longer horrified, but captivated. She picked it up and studied its odd symmetry. It was true. She had *never* created something like this before. It was sharp. It was so different from the flowers and lush green vines.

Isabela wasn't upset at all. She was amazed. Mirabel stepped back and watched as her sister delighted in creating something new, something different. She didn't seem mad anymore. She seemed downright gleeful. What was happening?

Isabela glided around her room, sprouting wild plants all along her path.

It turned out Isabela didn't need to make everything pretty. Isabela had been holding in her true self, and now that she had created something "not perfect," she felt free!

Mirabel followed her sister around the room, thinking that maybe these new plants were a sign. Maybe they meant something. Maybe she could *finally* embrace her sister, finish the vision, and save the magic!

But Isabela was too focused on her new creations.

Each new plant was an obstacle between Mirabel and her sister, but she followed Isabela as best as she could.

Soon Mirabel was being pushed and pulled around the room by bigger and more extravagant plants, all of them Isabela's weird and wonderful creations. Suddenly, a vine unraveled toward her, but Isabela pulled her onto the safety of a lush bed of green leaves.

Mirabel stood back and watched Isabela as she took in what she had created. She looked so full of wonder. This was a side of her sister she had never seen before. She smiled, admiring the outpouring of creativity and magic.

Their bed of leaves rose high into the air. It was a wax palm that shot straight through Isabela's bedroom ceiling, rushing the two sisters to the roof of Casita. They raced across the roof, and Mirabel spotted the candle in the courtyard below. It glowed brighter! Whatever Isabela was doing, the flame was growing stronger. Isabela excitedly continued to create amazing plant combinations with thorns, long vines, jagged leaves, and fierce waxy flowers like no one had ever seen before. Mirabel urged her on!

As hanging vines and prickly plants soared across the roof, the sisters grabbed each other, dived through a kaleidoscope of plants and flowers, and landed in a pile of lush petals, plants, and flowers in the courtyard. The two girls couldn't stop laughing. Isa glanced at Mirabel. She was grateful and happy! She moved in for a hug, when Abuela suddenly appeared in the courtyard.

"What have you done?!" she roared.

# chapter
# seventeen

Mirabel and Isabela sat up to see Abuela, with Tía Pepa in tow, staring at them. All of Isabela's wild plants had taken over the courtyard. Hearing the commotion, Mirabel's parents raced down from above. Mirabel glanced over to see that Isabela's perfect dress was now splattered with all sorts of vibrant colors. It looked beautiful! But under Abuela's stern gaze, Isabela went from joyful to ashamed. Mirabel gave her a supportive smile.

"Abuela, you don't understand. We made the candle brighter," Mirabel tried to explain.

"What are you talking about?!" Abuela cried.

"Look at your sister! Look at our home! Open your eyes!"

"Please just listen. . . . Isabela wasn't happy," Mirabel explained.

"Of course she wasn't happy. You ruined her proposal!"

"I found a way to help her. The candle burned brighter than I've ever seen. I was in the vision because I was supposed to help us."

"Mirabel." Abuela shook her head in disbelief.

"I'm supposed to save the magic. You just have to hear—"

"You have to stop, Mirabel!" Abuela warned. "The cracks started because of you."

Mirabel wasn't ready to back down. Was she the only one who truly had her eyes open? Why couldn't her abuela see the whole picture and what was happening to the family?

"No," Mirabel said. A sudden tremor rumbled under everyone's feet. The Encanto was breaking down.

"Bruno left our family because of you!" Abuela said. "Luisa's lost powers. Isabela's ruined proposal. I don't know why you weren't given a gift, but your refusal to accept it is breaking us! Our home is dying because of you!"

As Abuela continued to blame Mirabel, more cracks formed.

Mirabel could barely speak. She looked toward Isabela and Luisa and then back to her abuela. The pain of being blamed was worse than what she'd felt the night she didn't receive a gift. She thought about Tío Bruno and everything he had said. He had predicted that the family would turn the vision against her. He was right. This was why he'd kept it from all of them.

"You're wrong," Mirabel said softly as newly formed cracks led straight to Abuela. The candle started to flicker erratically as more cracks snaked across the floor and the walls, closing in on the candle. "Luisa will never be strong enough. Bruno isn't good enough. Isabela isn't perfect enough. And the night I didn't get a gift was . . . the night you stopped believing in me." Cracks rippled out between Mirabel and Abuela. "The house is dying because no one in this family is enough for you!"

"You have no idea what I've done for this family!" Abuela said.

"You have no idea what you've done *to* this family!"

"I have dedicated my life to protecting our family, our home."

Fissures surged throughout the Encanto. Alarmed by what was happening, the townspeople ran in fear to the Casa Madrigal for help.

"Open your eyes! Our family is falling apart because of you!" Mirabel argued.

Abuela was struck by Mirabel's strong words. But before she had a chance to respond, a large break nearly ripped the house apart as it snaked toward the candle. Mirabel watched with alarm as the house seemed helpless to what was happening to it. It let out a painful cry. Worse, the candle was now about to fall into a deep abyss.

"The candle! Save the candle!" Tía Pepa yelled.

The family swung into action. Isabela grabbed onto one of her vines to swoop the candle up and away from danger, but the vine disintegrated into dust, dropping her to the ground. Her prickly new plants that filled the courtyard disappeared as well.

"No!" Isabela screamed, her magic fading before her eyes.

The mountains surrounding the Encanto started to crack. The magic was dying too quickly, the cracks spreading faster and putting the whole village in danger. They had to get the candle *now*.

"Casita!" Mirabel cried, asking the house to help her once again. A railing from the balcony dropped down, giving Mirabel a way to climb up to the roof. She scrambled up as quickly as she could.

Meanwhile, the rest of the family tried to save the candle, too, but their magic was fading fast.

Camilo raced forward, changing shape in order to grab the candle, but as he reached out, he reverted to his normal self.

"Ah, no, no!" Camilo yelled.

Tía Pepa stepped in next, wielding her power over the weather to help.

"Pepi, amor, you have to stop the wind," Tío Felix urged her.

"I can't," she wailed. Her powers had vanished. She slumped down, defeated. Then she looked up, worried. "Where is Antonio?"

Dolores rushed to find Antonio and found him in his room. The giant tree in the middle of his room swayed and trembled. It was going to crush everything in its path. Antonio called to his animals for help, but they could no longer understand him.

Suddenly, the jaguar pulled Antonio and Dolores onto his back and raced them to safety just as the tree crashed through his door. The blast sent all of them flying.

"No!" Pepa screamed.

Tío Felix caught Antonio, and the house caught Dolores in a wheelbarrow. All the animals ran for their lives.

"Casita! You have to get everyone out! Do it now!" Mirabel yelled. As everyone's magic failed, the house used its remaining magic to usher the family out of harm's way.

"Vamos!" Tío Felix shouted as Luisa mustered the last bit of her strength to hold up a wooden beam while the family escaped. Agustín and Julieta helped her out from under the beam as her magic disappeared.

Inside the house, Bruno tried to escape from the hidden spaces of Casita. He put a bucket on his head and rammed through a wall. The house helped him, and he landed on a soft patch of grass, still unseen by his family. From the ground, he gazed up at the crumbling house.

"Vámonos todos, todos," Mirabel's father said, rushing everyone away from the house. "Come on, come on."

Mirabel hurried across the roof. There was still a way to save the candle. The candle was almost within reach when the roof released a sharp, aching whine. It was collapsing under her feet! It began to plummet when she nabbed the candle.

"Mirabel, no!" Julieta cried.

The house slid the roof tiles to push Mirabel out of the way and off the balcony as debris splattered down. In its final act of love, the house shielded Mirabel, saving her. Casita wheezed out dust, and the candle's flame went out.

"No," Mirabel whispered from the middle of

the rubble and dust. At her feet lay the broken remnants of their beautiful Casita. She reached through the rubble to pick up a piece of the house.

The home that she loved was gone.

From a distance, she heard the anguished voices of her family. She watched as Antonio said something to the toucan, but unable to understand him, it flew away.

"No wonder she didn't get a gift," someone said.

"Don't talk about Mirabel like that," another said.

"Don't talk to my son like that."

"There is no point in staying."

"Leave? How can we leave?"

"The Encanto is broken. She left us no choice."

Hearing the bickering, Mirabel walked off.

"Where is Mirabel? Mirabel?!" Julieta cried. Even as her mom called out for her, Mirabel knew that they were all better off without her.

By the time they turned to find her, Mirabel was gone.

# chapter
# eighteen

Mirabel trudged through the crumbled mountain pass. She reached the edge of a river and tripped, falling to the ground and ripping her dress. Catching her reflection in the water, Mirabel shook her head and winced. All she wanted was to make her family proud, and she had failed.

She took a seat on a rock to rest and get her bearings. She was leaving, but she wasn't quite sure where she was going.

"Mirabel," said a soft, familiar voice. Abuela made her way next to her. She had followed her from Casita.

"I'm sorry," Mirabel said, feeling ashamed. Her voice sounded tiny and broken. "I didn't want to hurt us. . . . I just wanted . . . to be something I'm not. . . ."

Abuela sat beside her, quiet and exhausted. Mirabel had never seen her abuela like this. She suddenly seemed so much older. For the first time, she seemed frail.

"I've never been able to come back here," Abuela said with a deep sadness. She gazed at the river like it was an old friend from her past. "This river is where we were given our miracle."

Mirabel looked at Abuela Alma. "Where Abuelo Pedro . . . ," she started, and Abuela nodded. Mirabel had no idea this was the river from all the stories about Abuelo Pedro and the night the Encanto was formed. What were the odds that she would find this place, tonight of all nights?

"I thought we would have a different life. . . . I thought I would be a different woman . . . ," Abuela explained. She looked back to the water as if the answers she needed were there, hidden beneath the surface. Mirabel peered in, too, and watched as her abuela's reflection transformed from that of an older woman to a young woman.

Through the rippled water, Abuela told the story of her and Abuelo Pedro.

In the small village where her abuela was raised, the people worked hard, and life was not easy. One day, Alma was carrying a large basket of food. Suddenly, the whinnying of horses ridden by dangerous men startled her, and she stumbled. Young Abuela dropped her basket at the feet of a young shop owner. Sensing trouble from the horsemen, the shop owner stepped forward and implored them to leave.

As they rode off, the young man helped Alma back to her feet and picked up her basket. That was the first time Mirabel's grandparents, Alma and Pedro, met.

Later, outside the shop, Pedro sewed a rip in Alma's dress. She watched him, her love growing stronger each minute they spent together. Although the village around them struggled, Alma and Pedro fell in love and were determined to stay together. They made plans and married.

On the steps of a small church, the newlyweds held a candle between them.

It was the same candle that was destroyed earlier this evening, the candle from which the Encanto grew. Mirabel understood for the first time that the magic candle had always been in the Madrigal family. Even before the magic, it was there shining its steady light on her abuelos' young love.

A few months later, young Alma was with Pedro in their modest home. She had just shared the news that she was pregnant—with triplets! Pedro pretended to faint, then grabbed her in an embrace.

The night the triplets were born, Pedro and Alma gazed down on them with true love, but then outside there was a large flash of light. Homes were ablaze, and sinister men who rode on horseback harassed the townspeople. The couple looked at their children and then back into each other's eyes. There was no choice—they had to leave and find a safer home.

Mirabel's abuelos packed everything they could. As they headed out the door, Pedro stopped and grabbed one more thing: the wedding candle. With the candle as their guide, Alma and Pedro set out into the night, followed by other families. They walked all night until they came to a river. It was the same river where Mirabel and Abuela Alma now sat.

With every step across the river, Pedro encouraged Alma to keep going. His words and loving eyes comforted her. Suddenly, there was a noise behind them. The sound of horses whinnying meant that the horsemen were coming. The whole group ran, scattering across the river. As chaos took over, Alma was frightened. What would happen to her babies? She held them tight. Pedro saw the fear in his wife's eyes and knew what he must do.

He gently lifted her face to his. His eyes told her everything would be okay. He kissed each one of his babies and then kissed Alma, full of love. He gazed into her eyes and made the promise that she would survive, she would thrive. Their children would find a new home and have a better life. Pedro kissed his wife one last time and raced toward the men on horseback. He tried to stop them and pled for his family's lives. Ruthlessly, the horsemen ignored his pleas, and in a flash . . . Pedro was gone.

As the other families panicked, Abuela looked to the river and then back to her babies. The men on horseback were closing in. She sank to her knees, heartbroken and frightened. She held on to the candle and begged the earth to spare the lives of her babies. She dug her hands into the wet soil. Suddenly, the ground around her began to glow, and the cruel horsemen were blown back by a mighty blast. The candle grew brighter and filled up with magic.

Abuela looked up to see that they were saved! The other families gathered around and stood in awe of what she had done. They began celebrating, but Alma stared out at the river where she last saw her beloved Pedro. As mountains magically rose up, the place where he died was covered forever.

Now young Abuela was alone and heartbroken in her bedroom in the new casa. She watched her tiny babies and realized she could not mourn forever. Her children needed her to be strong. She must fulfill the promise that Pedro had made. She must always work for a better life.

Just as Pedro had grabbed the candle to guide him that night, she grabbed the candle and placed it on her window. It would guide her, too. She stepped out her door, determined to make Pedro's sacrifice count.

As time went by and her children grew up, her grip on the family tightened, and so did her demands and expectations. Each member of the family had to make the Madrigals proud! They had to earn the miracle! In time, grandchildren were born, and each of them received a gift . . . except Mirabel.

After that night when the door faded for Mirabel, Abuela began to shun her. Then the cracks showed up, threatening everything Abuela had promised Pedro. Their home, their beautiful and spirited Casita, was now a pile of rubble, and the family was splintering and bickering.

Abuela could do nothing but hold tight to her chatelaine. She felt as if she had failed.

Abuela's voice brought Mirabel back to the present, where they gazed out across the river.

"I was given a miracle, a second chance, and I was so afraid to lose it that I lost sight of who his sacrifice was for," Abuela said with a defeated look. "If Pedro could see me now, he would be so disappointed."

She looked at Mirabel.

"You never hurt our family, Mirabel. We are broken because of me." As the words poured out, Abuela seemed shocked to have admitted it out loud.

Mirabel looked up at Abuela, understanding why she had been so hard and so strong for so long. She'd been through so much: she had fled her home, lost her husband, and raised three children by herself. After everything she had experienced, Abuela thought she had to protect the family. As they sat there, a butterfly fluttered onto a reed in the middle of the river.

Mirabel stared at it, transfixed. Where had she seen that butterfly before? The vision! Bruno had said to follow the butterfly. Mirabel had an idea. She took off her shoes and then unfastened Abuela's shoes as well. Holding hands, they waded out into the water together.

"Long ago, you and Abuelo had to flee your home," Mirabel said. They walked deeper into the river. "You carried so much for so long because there is nothing you care about more than our family. We were saved because of you. And there's no burden you ever need to carry by yourself again, because whatever comes our way, we will carry it with you."

As Abuela let Mirabel's words soak in, her heart opened. Suddenly, the sun peeked through the clouds, illuminating the river. Abuela looked at Mirabel in awe. She saw her clearly for the first time.

"I asked my Pedro for help. Mirabel, he sent me you," she said, oozing love and pride. She gently touched Mirabel's face. As Abuela embraced Mirabel, the water swirled and hundreds of butterflies rose up, fluttering about. Mirabel and her abuela watched them with tears streaming down their faces. As they held hands and returned to the riverbank, a loud commotion approached from the trees.

"She didn't do this!" Bruno yelled from atop a horse. He jumped down and confronted Abuela.

"I gave her a vision! It was me. I was like, go! And she was like, *fttttt!* She only wanted to help," he stammered breathlessly. "I . . . don't care what you think of me, but if you're too stubborn to, to just—"

Abuela silenced him with a long, loving embrace.

"Brunito," she said softly.

Bruno glanced at Mirabel, confused. "I feel like I've missed something important," he said.

"Come on!" Mirabel exclaimed, jumping on the horse. She helped Abuela up, then Bruno.

"What's happening? Where are we going?" Bruno asked.

"Home," Mirabel said. They raced off, following the trail of butterflies back to the Encanto.

# Chapter
# nineteen

Back at the ruins of Casita, darkness loomed over the land. The family and townspeople could do nothing but sit in shock at the destruction surrounding them. Mirabel's family were slumped over, dejected and unsure of what to do next. Their powers were gone! The house had collapsed. The whole town was crumbling. And Abuela and Mirabel were nowhere to be found.

Little Antonio, sitting atop his mom's shoulder, noticed a sparkling light. He tapped his mom gently and pointed to the immense light heading straight for them. Pepa looked up. It was Mirabel, riding a horse with Abuela clinging tight to her!

Tío Bruno was there, too! Behind them, a swarm of butterflies fluttered in a brilliant and magical light that pushed back the darkness. The family was stunned by the sight. The townspeople watched, awestruck.

Mirabel skidded to a stop in front of the ruined house. For a second, she was taken aback by the damage, but she didn't let it shake her.

"Mirabel!" her mom exclaimed. She grasped Mirabel in an embrace, relieved that her daughter was safe. "Ay, mi amor, I was so worried."

"Mamá, we're gonna be okay," Mirabel insisted.

Mirabel's family gathered around her as she began to share what she'd just seen and witnessed near the river. Abuela Alma joined in, bringing Tío Bruno into the family once more.

The family could hardly believe it. Bruno was back! And they were not afraid—they'd actually missed him so much! In all their stories about him, they had forgotten how soft-spoken and kind and creative he was.

One by one, each of them shared their sincere feelings, their fears and their desires. For the first time, they revealed their true selves. For so long, they hadn't really seen each other. But now their eyes were opened.

They started to pick up the rubble around them, piece by piece. The townspeople stepped forward, uncertain but wanting to help. The Madrigals quickly welcomed the help as they began to put Casita back together one stone, one wall, and one door at a time.

Handsome Mariano Guzmán rushed to Dolores's side and helped her. She smiled at him with a twinkle in her eyes. And as the family and townspeople worked through the night, the rubble began to look like Casita once again.

Once they were done, Mirabel and her family stood in front of their home to inspect their work. People started lighting candles, admiring the house in front of them. It was almost complete. There was just one thing missing.

Abuela handed Mirabel a final piece: a doorknob.

Mirabel stood in front of the doorway, catching her reflection in the doorknob she held in her hand.

She placed the doorknob in the door and *whoosh!* The house stirred back to life! Butterflies raced over the Encanto in a stream of twinkling light! As the families' powers were restored, Mirabel stood in front of the house. She smiled. Bruno's vision had come to pass.

The house waved at Mirabel. Mirabel waved back.

"Hola, Casita."

# epilogue

Magic returned to Casita, and the sun rose brightly over the Encanto once again. Abuela and Mirabel placed the candle back in the courtyard, where its magical glow pulsed brighter than ever! And it continued to remind the family not only of the sacrifice made for them, but of the fact that they shone because of their own worth. Not because of their gifts.

The family welcomed Tío Bruno with open arms, and he never had to eat dinner alone again. And the rat theater's stories of forbidden love were a hit with everyone!

Luisa continued to work hard, but she also

took "me time" whenever she wanted it. Isabela was now Señorita Perfecta of the most imperfect, wildest plants in town! And Dolores married the love of her life: handsome Mariano Guzmán! Their wedding ceremony was celebrated by the whole town. As for Mirabel . . .

One day, the family playfully blindfolded her for a special surprise. They chatted and laughed as they guided her through the house and to her bedroom door. When the family pulled the blindfold from Mirabel's eyes, she smiled from ear to ear! Each member of the family had decorated her door with something that reflected their own special gift. It was made from magic and glowed with love. Her very own special door!

Later in town, Mirabel played her accordion and shared the story of the miracle and the magical gifts with the children. And the children listened intently.

"A lot of people ask me about my family, and I always tell them the same thing: our family is exactly like *your* family."

"Was everyone really blessed with a magical gift?" Mirabel continued. "Well, sometimes our gifts are harder to see than others'—sometimes our gifts are different than you might think. And *sometimes,* if you look really close . . . if you open your eyes . . . you just might find you'll never have one . . . ," Mirabel said. "Wait, no, sorry— you never *needed* one. You get the idea!"

Then, *poof!* A new family portrait was taken. In it, everyone posed with their goofiest face. And the best part? It was hung on the family wall. Mirabel was no longer unseen. She was right in the middle of the family portrait . . . where she belonged.